# THE SHOW MUST GO ON

Tragedy dogs the footsteps of three ex-soldiers — Clifford, Ronnie and Keith — when they start to produce a show planned in their Army days. The theatre they lease is reputed to be haunted since an actor, Castleton Mayne, was murdered on the stage thirty years before . . . On their first visit, the son of the owner, Alexander Mayne, is mysteriously murdered. Then a rival producer, in league with the displaced leading lady, tries his utmost to ruin the show . . .

GERALD VERNER

# THE SHOW MUST GO ON

*Complete and Unabridged*

# LINFORD
*Leicester*

First published in Great Britain

First Linford Edition
published 2015

Copyright © 1950 by Gerald Verner
Copyright © 2015 by Chris Verner

A catalogue record for this book is available
from the British Library.

ISBN 978–1–4448–2629–6

Published by
F. A. Thorpe (Publishing)
Anstey, Leicestershire

Set by Words & Graphics Ltd.
Anstey, Leicestershire
Printed and bound in Great Britain by
T. J. International Ltd., Padstow, Cornwall

This book is printed on acid-free paper

For Christopher Stuart

# 1

The stage of the Rialto Theatre in Shaftesbury Avenue was dimly lit. The light spread faintly over the empty orchestra pit and as far as the front row of the stalls, but the vast cavern of the auditorium stretched away into shadows and ultimate darkness, the lines of sheeted seats like the waves of a frozen sea.

On the stage a girl was singing, in front of a jigging line of other women, to the accompaniment of a piano pushed up against one side of the proscenium. She was singing a bright, catchy number, swaying her slim hips to the music and smiling into the echoing darkness in front of her.

Down in the stalls, where one of the dust-sheets had been pulled aside, a man watched and listened critically. He was a lean man with a thin, bronzed face, and hair that was going a little grey at the sides of his well-shaped head; a pleasant-faced man in spite of the deep lines about his mouth.

He clapped his hands together sharply and the singer, the jigging chorus, and the piano all stopped abruptly.

'Just a minute,' he called, getting up and moving to the orchestra rail. 'You'll have to come farther downstage, Miss Sheringham — so will you, girls. Otherwise you'll get in the way of the tabs . . . '

The girl who had been singing came nearer to the footlights.

'Oh, I see, Mr. Brett,' she said. 'I'm sorry.'

'It's difficult to tell how much room you've got until we get the tabs up,' said Clifford Brett. 'Victor . . . '

'Yes, Mr. Brett?' A small, dapper man appeared from the left-hand side of the stage and peered down into the stalls.

'Can you show 'em where those tabs 'ull go?' asked Brett.

The stage manager nodded.

'You're using the second set for this number, aren't you?' he said.

'Yes.'

'Well, they'll come here.' Victor Price picked up a chair and set it down upstage.

'That's the deadline, Miss Sheringham,' he said. 'You can't come farther back than that.'

'I see,' said the girl.

'That applies to all of you,' said Brett. 'All right? We'll go through that number again, then . . . Ready, Keith?'

The dark, good-looking man at the piano nodded. The chorus girls disappeared into the shadows at the side of the dark stage to await their cue, and Maysie Sheringham took up her position in the centre of the stage. The piano tinkled out an introduction and the number began.

Brett let it go through to the end without interruption, and then he said: 'That was better — much better. Don't crowd it though, girls — keep well spread out behind Miss Sheringham and keep your line . . . You, my dear, in blue — what's your name?'

'Tangye — Tangye Ward,' answered the fair girl he had spoken to. She was very pretty and there was intelligence in her large grey eyes.

'Listen, Tangye,' Brett continued. 'When the other girls form that semicircle at the end of the number, don't come so far down.'

'All right, Mr. Brett,' she said.

'That's all,' he said. 'O.K. everybody — we'll break for lunch now. Back at two o'clock sharp, please.'

There was a general movement from the people who had been standing or sitting about the bare stage and a buzzing chatter of voices. As Brett came up the short flight of steps that led up to the stage from the auditorium a tall woman moved languidly forward to meet him.

'Oh, Mr. Brett,' she said in a rather affected voice, 'need I come back at two? I've rather an important appointment . . . '

'I wanted to try over that number with you, Miss Peters.' The good-looking man who had been playing the piano came quickly over to them.

'Couldn't we do it some other time, Mr. Gilbert?' said Madeleine Peters. 'I'm lunching with Mr. Defoe and I can't possibly be back by two . . . '

'Well . . . ' Keith Gilbert was beginning when Brett broke in.

'All right, Miss Peters, but get back as soon as you can,' he said.

'Thank you, Mr. Brett,' she said, not very graciously and walked away.

Keith Gilbert looked after her with an expression of dislike.

'The airs that woman puts on make me sick,' he declared.

'I know,' agreed Brett, 'but we've got to put up with her. Defoe would never have let us have this theatre if we hadn't agreed to star Madeleine Peters, and there's no other theatre available . . . '

'I wouldn't care if she were good,' grunted Keith, 'but she isn't. That girl you were talking to just now — Tangye-what's-her-name? — can sing her into a cocked hat . . . '

'Tangye Ward hasn't got a boyfriend who owns theatres, Keith,' retorted Brett. He looked round as a woman's high-heeled shoes echoed on the bare boards of the stage. 'Hello, here's Miss Winter. I wonder what she wants . . . '

The woman who hurried over to them

5

was middle-aged and thin. Her hair, once a dark brown, was streaked with grey and her nose jutted out from between high cheekbones. Her eyes, of a curious light blue so that they looked almost sightless, were tired and strained. She carried a large envelope under one arm.

'Mr. Brett,' she said breathlessly, as she joined them, 'Mr. Macdonald asked me to bring you these sketches . . . Miss Sigorski left them at the office half an hour ago . . . ' She took the envelope from under her arm and held it out.

'Oh, thank you,' said Brett. He took the envelope and looked round. 'Where's Ronnie?' he asked.

'He was here a moment ago,' said Keith. 'There he is — over there, talking to Nutty. Ronnie . . . Ronnie!'

'You want me?' A pleasant-faced, fairish man with a little smear of moustache above his upper lip hurried over. 'What is it? Oh, good morning, Miss Winter . . . '

'Good morning, Mr. Hays.'

'Here are the sketches for those finale dresses,' said Brett. He took them out of the envelope. 'See what you think of 'em . . . '

'I must go back to the office, Mr. Brett,' broke in Olivia Winter. 'Have you any message for Mr. Macdonald?'

'No, I don't think so.' answered Brett, shaking his head. 'I'll be seeing him later . . . Thanks for bringing these sketches.'

'That's all right, Mr. Brett,' she said and, nodding to the other two, hurried away. The little man to whom Ronnie Hays had been talking came over.

'Wotcher got there?' he asked.

'The designs for the finale dresses,' said Hays. 'They're very good, Clifford.'

'Natalie Sigorski's designs are always good,' said Brett. 'She handles colour so well . . . I thought you were going to take Maysie Sheringham out to lunch, Nutty?'

'So did I,' replied the little man, with a grimace, 'but she 'ad other ideas. She's a smashin' bit of 'omework, ain't she? Cor lumme! She's got everythin' . . . '

'Including a luncheon date apparently,' remarked Brett. 'Never mind, Nutty — you'll have to put up with us. Let's go over the road for a drink and a snack at the bar, shall we?'

Almost opposite the stage door of the Rialto Theatre there is a pub with a long bar at which you can obtain a very appetizing meal. In the days before austerity became one of the chief characteristics of the British Isles there used to be a noble ham, brown with breadcrumbs, from which George, the barman, would skilfully cut succulent slices to go with the salads and other delicacies so temptingly displayed. The ham, alas, has disappeared, together with the mighty Stilton. There is, however, still a fair choice and, in consequence, the place is very popular.

It was too early for the bar to have filled up when Brett and the others entered and they easily found stools at the counter.

'Wot yer goin' ter 'ave?' demanded Nutty Potts hospitably.

'Now, look here, Nutty,' said Clifford Brett, 'you're not going to do this again . . .'

'Course I am,' retorted Nutty. 'Now

what is it? Tell me wot yer goin' to drink an' then we can talk about the grub . . . '

'No, Nutty,' said Keith Gilbert. 'You did it all yesterday . . . '

'Well, what about it?' said the little man. 'I can do it again if I want, can't I? Wot yer got terday, George?'

'Very nice chicken salad, sir.'

'That'll do me,' said Brett.

'Sounds good to me, too,' said Keith.

'I'd rather have cheese, I think,' said Hays. 'But without cucumber, please . . . '

'Chicken for me,' said Nutty. 'Now what about these drinks? Give 'em a name and I'll go an' get 'em.'

They argued with him but he was insistent.

'Oh, well,' said Ronnie Hays, 'if you *will* buy them I'd better come and help you carry.'

He followed the little man over to the bar and Brett looked at Gilbert and shrugged his shoulders helplessly.

'What can you do?' he murmured. 'Nutty's a good chap but I do wish he wouldn't always insist on paying for everything . . . '

'He gets annoyed if you don't let him,' said Keith. 'After all you don't win seventy thousand pounds in a football pool every day. That was an amazing bit of luck for him, wasn't it?'

'Yes — and for us,' said Brett. 'If Nutty hadn't agreed to back us there'd have been no show ... Do you remember when we first planned it, Keith? You and I and Ronnie — in Alamein with the shells from Rommel's guns screaming round us ... '

'And our mouths full of sand and flies by the million ... ' Keith Gilbert nodded, his eyes full of memories. 'Ronnie used to scribble lyrics on any odd scraps of paper he could get hold of and I'd hum tunes to fit 'em ... We said if we ever got back we'd do a show together ... '

'And it's all come true ... thanks to Nutty.'

'Good old Nutty,' said Keith.

Nutty and Ronnie Hays came back with the drinks, the little man beaming all over his rugged face.

''Ere yer are, Mr. Brett,' he said, handing Brett a foaming pint tankard of beer. 'Whisky an' soda fer you, Mr. Gilbert . . . '

'Why don't you drop the 'mister', Nutty,' said Brett. 'You're not my batman now, you know.'

'Old 'abits die 'ard,' grinned Nutty. 'Cor blimey! Wot we wouldn't 'ave given fer a pint o' luvverly cool beer in North Africa, eh?'

'We've just been talking about that,' said Brett. 'Remember how you used to scrounge all the bits of paper you could, Nutty?'

'Course I do . . . I nearly got a black eye from Corporal 'Ancock fer pinchin' that letter from 'is best girl . . . '

Ronnie laughed.

'I wrote 'Country Air' on that,' he said.

'An' the time I got yer that writin' pad,' continued Nutty. 'There wasn't 'alf a flamin' row about *that* . . . '

'Yes — there isn't a page of the script that hasn't got a story attached to it,' remarked Brett.

'Let's hope it's going to be a success story,' said Keith.

'It's just got to be,' said Brett. 'Up to now I'm very pleased at the way it's shaping at rehearsals . . .'

'Except for Madeleine Peters,' said Keith, with a grimace.

'We can't do anything about that,' said Clifford Brett. 'We've got to put up with her if we want the Rialto, and without it we'd be sunk.'

'How she ever became a star is beyond my comprehension,' said Hays, and Brett shrugged his shoulders.

'Phillip Defoe's influence,' he said. 'He forced her down the public's throat.'

''E's a nasty piece o' work,' grunted Potts, swirling the beer round his tankard. 'I wouldn't trust that bloke with a kid's money-box.'

'Look,' interrupted Keith Gilbert, 'there's that girl Tangye — Tangye Ward — just come in. She's all by herself — let's call her over . . .'

There was no need. The girl had already seen them and came over with a smile.

'Hello,' she said.

'Hello,' said Keith. He pulled out one

of the red-leather stools. 'Sit down . . . '

'Wot yer goin' ter 'ave, Miss?' asked Nutty.

'That's very nice of you, Mr. Potts.' She smiled down at him from the high stool. 'I'd like a shandy, please . . . '

'An' a nice bit o' chicken salad, eh?' he suggested.

She shook her head.

'You might as well, Tangye,' put in Keith. 'Nutty'll be horribly offended if you don't . . . '

'Oh, well . . . all right, then — I will,' she said.

'That's right — 'ave a bash,' said Nutty, and called to the barman. 'Let's 'ave another chicken salad, will yer, chum?'

'Yes, sir,' answered George.

'Now I'll just 'op over an' get yer shandy an' we'll be okey doke.' He grinned and went over to the bar.

'Nutty's thoroughly enjoying himself,' remarked Hays.

'I think he's a dear,' said the girl.

'One of the best, old Nutty,' said Brett. 'How do you like the show, Tangye?'

'Very much. Is it true that you wrote it

while you were in the army?'

'Yes, most of it,' answered Hays. 'We've added a few numbers, but the bulk of the stuff was done in North Africa.'

'How did you manage it in the middle of all — all that?'

'Well, Jerry was a bit of a nuisance at times,' admitted Hays.

'He started shelling us once when Ronnie was trying to find a rhyme for 'lasted',' said Keith.

'I gather he found it?' she said.

'He did,' agreed Keith, 'but it was hardly — er — suitable for a sentimental lyric.'

She laughed. Keith thought that she looked very attractive when she laughed. Her nose wrinkled and there were two dimples that formed little half-moons at the sides of her mouth.

The barman began setting plates before them and Nutty came back with the shandy. They ate and drank and chatted about the show. Clifford Brett bought another round of drinks, after an argument with Nutty Potts, who tried to get in first, and then, during a momentary

14

lull in the conversation Keith Gilbert said:

'By the way, Clifford, has Defoe actually signed the contract for the Rialto yet?'

'No. we've signed our half, but he hasn't signed his — at least his solicitors haven't sent it back yet.'

'It's a lovely theatre, isn't it?' said Tangye. 'I've always wanted to be with a show at the Rialto.'

'Haven't you ever played there before?' asked Keith.

'No,' she answered. 'I rehearsed once for one of Mr. Defoe's productions, but . . . well, I didn't open.'

'What happened?' inquired Hays.

Her brow clouded and she pursed her lips.

'It was Miss Peters,' she explained. 'She didn't like me and so — I got my notice . . . '

'I see . . . ' Brett nodded.

'She's done the same to a lot of girls,' Tangye went on quickly. 'If she doesn't like you — well, you don't stay, that's all.'

'Yes, I can quite believe that,' said Keith.

There was a short silence and then Tangye said, hesitantly:

'Look — perhaps I shouldn't say this . . . It's none of my business really, but . . . if you're doing any business with Phillip Defoe you want to be very careful.'

'How do you mean?' asked Brett.

'Well . . .' She was a little reluctant to continue. 'He's very smart . . . He'll twist you if he can . . .'

'I don't see how he can twist us very easily,' said Brett. 'We have got the Rialto on a rental basis with a share of the gross box office receipts. He can't do much jiggery-pokery about that, can he?'

She looked at him thoughtfully and it was some time before she replied.

'No,' she said at last, slowly. 'No, perhaps he can't, but . . . but all the same, Mr. Brett, watch your step — do watch your step!'

★　★　★

The dark, good-looking man sitting opposite Madeleine Peters at a table in

16

the Milan grill-room, glanced at his watch.

'Had you not better be getting back, my dear?' he said, speaking with a slight and rather attractive foreign accent.

'There's plenty of time, Phillip,' she said, 'let them wait. I want another brandy.'

'We don't want any trouble — yet, Madeleine,' said Phillip Defoe, softly.

'There won't be any trouble,' she answered scornfully. 'They daren't say anything to me, you know that . . . Order me another brandy, there's a darling.'

He shrugged immaculate shoulders — everything about him was immaculate and smooth — and signalled to a waiter.

'Yes, sir?'

'Bring two more cognacs.'

'Yes, sir.'

The waiter hurried away and Defoe took out a cigarette-case and offered it to Madeleine.

'You know,' he said as she took a cigarette, 'they've got the making of a good show. Hays has got some clever ideas and Gilbert's music is very tuneful . . . '

'It's not bad . . . '

'It's very good.' He flicked a lighter into flame and held it to her cigarette. 'It's very good indeed. I realized how good it was when they first approached me about the Rialto. I think it will be a big success, but . . . ' He stopped and lit his own cigarette.

'Well? Go on. But — what?' she demanded.

'Why should it be a success for them?' he asked.

'What are you getting at?' She stared at him with puzzled eyes.

The waiter arrived with a bottle of brandy and two fresh glasses. Warming them over a little spirit lamp he poured out the brandy, bowed, and went away.

'I've lost a lot of money lately, my dear,' said Defoe, swirling the brandy gently round in the big warm glass and inhaling the bouquet appreciatively. 'More than I like losing. My last two productions were not financial successes.'

She stared at him with wide eyes. It was

a trick she had practised for hours before her mirror and it was quite effective.

'I always thought . . . ' she began.

'You always thought they were?' He nodded. 'I don't believe in advertising failures,' he said. 'It is not good for business. But I want to get that money back. Why shouldn't I get it out of this show?'

'Because it's not yours . . . ' began Madeleine.

'But it might easily become mine,' he interrupted.

'How?'

'They have spent a lot of money these three,' he said, dropping his voice.

'You mean that awful man Potts has,' she said, spitefully. '*They* haven't any money . . . '

'It's the same thing — they won't want to see him lose it . . . '

'How is he going to lose? Unless the show's a flop . . . '

'I see you do not understand,' he said. 'Listen — they have ordered all the scenery. It is being built and painted now. They have ordered most of the dresses, and the entire cast has been engaged and have received their contracts — they are committed for thousands of pounds . . . '

'Yes, I know all that,' she said, impatiently, 'but . . . '

'If anything stopped the show going on, the greater part of that money would be lost . . . ' He paused and looked at her steadily.

'I still don't get it,' she said.

'Supposing they don't get the Rialto Theatre after all?' said Defoe. 'Supposing at the last moment I change my mind and refuse to let them have it? There's no other theatre available and there won't be for months . . . '

'But they've signed the contract . . . '

'They have, Madeleine, but I haven't,' he said. 'And there's a clause in that agreement that makes the whole thing conditional on *you* being the star . . . '

'Well, I am,' she said, quickly.

'At present,' he agreed. 'But supposing, in a week or so, for some reason or other you walked out? Quite legitimately I can refuse to allow them to have the Rialto.'

'Perhaps you could, Phillip,' she said,

'but what good would it do you?'

Defoe took the cigarette from his lips, blew out a cloud of smoke, and leaned forward.

'They can't open,' he said slowly. 'There's no other theatre to get. They're landed with the scenery, the dresses, the cast — all useless to them. They've got to pay out a great deal of money without the prospect of any return. Right! Then I offer to take over the whole production, lock, stock and barrel, for a nominal sum . . . Don't you think they'd jump at the offer and cut their losses? The show goes on at the Rialto, but under my management — and I get it for next to nothing . . . Do you understand *now*?'

She looked at him and there was admiration in her eyes.

'Phillip,' she said, softly, 'you're as clever and cunning as the devil . . . '

# 2

'More tea, Maysie?' asked Tangye.

Maysie Sheringham closed up her compact and put it back in her handbag.

'Please,' she said, 'if there is any . . . '

'There's heaps. I don't know whether it's very strong, though.'

'I don't mind a bit . . . '

Tangye poured out a cup of tea that was at least faintly coloured. The two girls were sitting in a tea-shop in a street off Shaftesbury Avenue. They had just finished rehearsing for that day and both looked a little tired.

'The show's going quite well, isn't it?' said Maysie, searching in her bag for a cigarette.

'Except for that Peters woman,' answered Tangye.

'Oh, she's a cat . . . she's always the same.' Maysie found a crumpled packet of Players and offered one to Tangye.

'Thanks,' said Tangye, taking a cigarette. 'I don't think she's ever been quite so bad as this. The way she's behaving you'd think she was trying to pick a quarrel, wouldn't you?'

'I don't see what object she could have for doing *that*,' said Maysie. 'I think she's just being very Madeleine Peterish, and a bit more than usual . . . Have you got a match? My lighter wants filling . . . '

'Try mine.' Tangye produced it from her bag. 'It's a shame — because they're awfully nice . . . '

'*All* of them, darling?' murmured Maysie mischievously, her eyes twinkling over the flame of the lighter.

'I don't know what you mean,' said Tangye.

'I thought perhaps you thought one was a little bit nicer than the others,' said Maysie, demurely.

'I think they're all nice,' said Tangye, a little defiantly.

'They are.' Maysie took a sip of tea and made a wry face. 'I wish that little man, Potts, wouldn't follow me about quite so much . . . '

'He's rather a dear . . . '

'He's always asking me to go to lunch with him, or tea, or dinner. He doesn't seem to have an idea above his stomach.'

'Why don't you go?' said Tangye.

'I might — if he hadn't got all that money . . . '

'What difference does that make?'

'People might get erroneous ideas,' said Maysie. 'I'd hate to be thought another Madeleine Peters . . . '

Tangye laughed.

'I'm sure poor Nutty thinks you just don't like him,' she said.

'I think he's rather sweet, really. He reminds me of a little dog I once had . . . '

'Maysie!'

'Well, he does,' declared Maysie. 'It's something in the way he looks at you . . . '

'Not at *me*.'

'At me, then . . . with those big eyes and his head slightly on one side. It might be Bingo . . . '

'Poor Nutty,' said Tangye.

'I was very fond of Bingo,' said Maysie. She flicked her ash into a saucer. 'I hope the show will be a success. It ought to be, if Peters doesn't ruin it. She's trying her best . . . '

'I don't think they'll stand much more from her,' said Tangye.

'In that case, darling,' remarked Maysie, 'we can all go and look for new jobs. They daren't say much to her, Tangye. If they lose the Rialto they stand about as much chance of getting another theatre as as I do of playing Lady Macbeth.'

'Oh, well, maybe it will work out all right,' said Tangye, hopefully. 'I should hate anything to go wrong . . . They've put so much into this show. They planned it in Alamein and wrote most of it there, too. They told me about it . . . only a little . . . but I could picture the rest . . . what they *didn't* tell me . . . '

'I know,' Maysie nodded. 'I'd hate anything to go wrong, too. Well, we'd better go. I've got some smalls to wash, and I want an early night . . . '

They paid the bill and walked together as far as Piccadilly Circus, where Maysie caught a bus. Tangye, as she made her way down to the Tube, found that she was still worrying about the behaviour of the unpleasant Miss Peters. What happened on the following day proved that her worry had not been without cause . . .

★   ★   ★

The morning rehearsal was over. The rest of the company had gone their various ways for lunch, but Keith Gilbert and Madeleine Peters had stayed behind to try over a new number which Gilbert had written on the previous night. Four times Madeleine had been through it, but Keith was still not satisfied.

'Could we try it again, please?' he said.

'What, *again?*' she protested. 'I'm a little tired and I want my lunch . . . '

'I'm sorry,' said Keith stubbornly, 'I won't keep you much longer.'

He played the introduction and she began to sing. Half-way through the refrain he stopped her.

'Can't you put more feeling into it, Miss Peters?' he said. 'As if it really meant something to you . . . '

'It doesn't mean a thing to me,' she said, crossly. 'I don't like the number.'

'What's the matter with it?' he asked.

'Everything,' she retorted. 'It doesn't suit me . . . '

'That's obvious,' said Keith, 'but there's nothing wrong with the number . . . '

'That's a matter of opinion,' she said.

'It's a sentimental number, but the way you're singing it, it might as well be the multiplication table!'

'How dare you speak to me like that!' she said, furiously.

'There's no need to lose your temper . . . ' he began, but she broke in:

'What am I supposed to do?' she demanded. Say 'yes, Mr. Gilbert' when you tell me — me, who's starred in all Phillip Defoe's productions — that I don't know how to put a number over . . . '

'I didn't say that . . . '

'Yes, you did — or as good as . . . '

'But you must realize, Miss Peters,' said Gilbert, trying to control his rising temper, 'that the number is wrong . . . '

'Is that my fault?' she flared angrily. 'Of course the number's wrong — the lyrics are wrong and the music's worse . . . You can tear the thing up. I *won't* sing it . . . '

'I'm afraid you'll have to,' he said quietly.

'Oh, shall I? Well, let me tell you that I absolutely refuse . . . That number comes out, d'you hear?'

'I hear,' he answered, 'but the number stays in, Miss Peters.'

For a moment she was almost speechless with rage. Any attraction she may have possessed had disappeared with the veneer of refinement.

'Very well,' she said, huskily, after a pause. 'Then I quit. You can find somebody else to sing your lousy music . . . I quit, d'you understand?' Her voice rose shrilly. 'We'll see what Phillip Defoe has to say to *that*!'

She turned and flounced away, almost knocking over Ronnie Hays as he came through the door leading to the stage. Keith Gilbert, his face red and set, got up abruptly and slammed down the lid of the piano.

'I say,' said Hays, 'what's the matter with La Peters?'

'We've just had a row,' answered Gilbert. 'I didn't like the way she sang that new number . . . I told her I didn't . . . she lost her temper and walked out.'

Ronnie Hays uttered a low whistle.

'What's going to happen now?' he demanded.

'Don't ask me . . . ' Keith shook his head. 'She'll probably come back when she's got over it.'

There was a patter of high heels on the bare stage and they turned, thinking that Madeleine Peters had came back. But it was Tangye.

'Hello,' she greeted, and then: 'What's the matter? You both look very worried . . . '

'Madeleine Peters has walked out,' said Keith.

'Do you mean she's left the show?' asked Tangye, quickly.

They nodded.

'So she says . . . ' began Hays, and stopped as the voice of Clifford Brett hailed them.

'Nobody else back yet?' he called. 'It's two o'clock . . . Hello, what's the matter?' His eyes searched their faces questioningly. They told him what had happened and he looked grave.

'D'you think she means it?' he asked.

'She was in a flaming temper,' said Keith.

The rest of the company began to arrive and Brett shrugged his shoulders.

'We'll have to get on with the rehearsal without her,' he said. 'Nuisance . . . I wanted to begin with that opening number of hers . . . '

'I know it,' said Tangye, quickly. 'I'll take her place for now, if you like, Mr. Brett.'

'That's fine.' His face cleared. 'All right, Victor, call the girls. We're going to do the opening number. Miss Ward will take the place of Miss Peters for now . . . '

'Everybody concerned in the opening number, stand by,' called the stage manager. The laughing and the chattering ceased, Keith took his place at the piano, and the rehearsal started. Tangye sang the number very well, and Keith gave her an encouraging smile when she finished.

'That was really good,' he said.

Hays, who was leaning on the back of the piano, nodded.

'Better than Madeleine Peters ever sang it,' he murmured.

'Or ever could,' said Keith. 'Hello . . . here's Defoe . . . '

Hays followed the direction of his eyes and frowned. Phillip Defoe had entered from the back of the stalls and was walking down the centre gangway towards Clifford Brett. His face was set and he looked coldly angry.

'There's going to be trouble, I think,' whispered Hays.

'Mr. Brett!' Defoe called to Clifford Brett, curtly.

'Oh . . . good afternoon, Mr. Defoe . . . '

'I'm afraid you will have to find somewhere else to rehearse your show,' continued Defoe. 'I require this theatre . . . '

'I don't understand . . . You said we could rehearse here,' began Brett, and Defoe stopped him with a gesture.

'That was when we were discussing the

possibility of my renting this theatre for the production of your revue,' said Defoe.

'Now wait a minute,' protested Brett. 'There was no 'possibility' — it was all fixed . . . '

'The contract has not been signed,' replied Defoe. 'I have instructed my solicitors not to proceed further with it!'

'But you can't do that,' said Brett in dismay.

'I not only can, but I have,' replied Defoe. 'My offer of the Rialto Theatre was conditional upon Miss Peters being the star in your show . . . Miss Peters tells me that she has resigned from the cast.'

'She walked out in a temper . . . '

'It does not concern me how or why she left, Mr. Brett. She is no longer in the cast — that is all that matters.'

Clifford Brett bit his lip. He would have liked to smash his fist into the cold, sneering face of the man before him, but with an effort he controlled himself.

'Look here,' he said, 'let's talk this over . . . '

'There is nothing to talk over,' said the other shortly. 'I require my theatre. Will you please arrange that all these people are out of it as soon as possible. Good afternoon.'

He turned on his heel and without another word walked back up the gangway and out of the exit door.

# 3

Macdonald's Theatrical Agency occupies the third floor of a large block of offices in Charing Cross Road. When you step out of the lift, if you are lucky enough to find it working, the door of the outer office bearing the legend 'Inquiries' faces you. If you open this door you will find yourself in a small room bisected by a counter behind which sits a very thin and very pimply youth, generally immersed in a copy of one of those lurid-covered novels that can be purchased from the bookstalls for one and sixpence and are worth less than nothing. Having passed this outpost of Empire, or maybe you are more concerned with the Hippodrome, you will come to a larger office presided over by Olivia Winter. If you are a manager, a star, or some equally very important person, you may eventually reach the holy of holies and the great Angus Macdonald himself. If this remarkable piece of good fortune should happen to you, you will find yourself in the presence of a large and angular man with an almost completely bald head. A few wisps of reddish hair surround this dome of skin-covered bone, but there is less of it than goes to make up the rather bushy eyebrows. Mr. Macdonald is very Scottish. His accent is so thick that only the very sharpest of knives would cut it.

On this particular afternoon Mr. Macdonald is in conference. He is also on the telephone. Facing him, grouped round the large and imposing desk, from behind which Mr. Macdonald is wont to awe his less influential clients, are Clifford Brett, Keith Gilbert, Ronnie Hays, and Nutty Potts. They are all looking very worried and depressed, as well they may, for there is a crisis on hand.

' . . . ye canna suggest anything?' grunted Macdonald into the telephone. 'I was afraid ye couldna, but I thought I'd just ring ye up on the off-chance . . . Aye, I noo . . . Goodbye to ye . . . '

He hung up the receiver and slowly shook his large naked head.

'No luck?' asked Brett.

'No,' replied Macdonald. 'I fear ye'll no get a theatre, Brett. It's the same story everywhere. There's a boom, ye see.'

Clifford Brett tapped impatiently on the desk.

'We've got to do something,' he declared. 'Can't you think of *anything*, Mac?'

Again Macdonald shook his head.

'I've tried everybody,' he said.

'We can't afford to postpone the production,' Brett continued. 'We're going to lose thousands if we don't open . . . of Nutty's money.'

'Don't yer go worryin' about that, Mr. Brett,' put in the little man cheerfully. 'It ain't your fault . . . '

'I suppose it's mine, really,' said Keith. 'Look here — let me go and apologize to Madeleine Peters . . . '

'No,' snapped Brett, curtly, 'you can't do that . . . '

'Apologize to 'er?' cried Nutty. 'Cor blimey, I should blinkin' well say not . . . '

'You're sure there isn't somewhere we've overlooked?' asked Ronnie Hays.

'I canna think of anywhere,' said Macdonald.

'We've got to find somewhere,' declared Brett. 'We can't let all these people down. They've been rehearsing for over a week . . . ' He got up and began to pace the office restlessly.

'What can ye do?' Macdonald shrugged his shoulders. 'Ye canna produce a theatre that doesna exist by wishful thinking . . . '

'Couldn't we take the show on tour?' suggested Hays.

'The same thing applies,' said Macdonald. 'The number one and two dates are all booked up. We'd no be able to get a consecutive tour . . . '

'It looks as if we was sunk,' remarked Nutty.

'Aye — ye canna make bricks without straw . . . '

'Then we've got to find the straw,' said Brett. 'We've got to go on until we find a way out.'

'Ye're a fine optimist, I will say that for ye,' remarked Macdonald

'It's the only thing that's going to help.' Brett stopped at the window and drummed his fingers on the glass. 'There must be somewhere we can get . . . '

Nobody answered him. With gloomy faces they stared in front of them, racking their brains fruitlessly to find a solution. Suddenly the drumming sound of Brett's fingers on the pane stopped and he uttered an exclamation.

'I've got it!' he almost shouted. 'Why didn't I think of it before? The Regency!'

'The Regency?' Keith Gilbert looked at him questioningly.

'Yes,' said Brett, coming back to the desk and leaning on it. 'The old theatre in Oxford Street . . . '

'But, mon, it's been closed for over thirty years,' cried Macdonald.

'What does that matter?' said Brett quickly. 'We'll re-open it.'

'Ye're crazy! It'll be in a terrible state . . . '

'We can have it cleaned and redecorated,' Brett waved aside the objection impatiently. 'Who does it belong to?'

'It belongs to the Maynes,' answered Macdonald. 'Isobel Mayne and her son Alexander, but ye'll no get permission from *them* to re-open it, I'm thinkin'.'

'Why not?'

'Do ye not know the story connected with it?'

'Story?'

'Ye've heard, no doubt, of Castleton Mayne?'

'The Shakespearian actor?'

'Aye,' said Macdonald, nodding thoughtfully, 'the *great* Shakespearian actor. His Hamlet was the best performance ever seen on any stage . . .'

'Wait a minute,' interrupted Hays, frowning. 'I've read something somewhere about Mayne. He was murdered or something, wasn't he?'

'He was murdered,' said Macdonald, 'on the stage of the Regency Theatre during a performance of *Hamlet*. Marsden, who was playing Laertes, stabbed him in the throat. He was jealous of Mayne's success. He died a year later, raving mad, in an asylum.'

'And the theatre's been shut up ever since?' asked Keith.

'Mrs. Mayne closed it,' answered Macdonald. 'The tragic death of her husband upset her mind, poor soul — she was devoted to him . . . '

'D'yer mean — she's crackers?' asked Potts.

Macdonald nodded.

'As crazy as — as Ophelia, the part she was playing when it happened. They call the Regency the haunted theatre.'

'Why?' demanded Brett.

'Well . . . ' Macdonald hesitated, pulling at his large nose. 'There have been some queer stories . . . '

'If we can get the place a few ghosts won't worry me,' said Brett. 'How can we get hold of the Maynes?'

'I'm no certain of the address,' answered Macdonald. 'We have it in the office somewhere, I'm thinkin'.' He pressed a button on his desk. 'We'll ask Miss Winter . . . '

'We ought to get a lot of publicity re-opening a theatre that's been closed for thirty years,' said Brett.

'Ye've no got it yet,' remarked Macdonald. 'Dinna count your chickens . . . '

'We've got to get it,' said Brett. 'The Regency's our only hope. We'll persuade

40

Mrs. Mayne to let us have it, don't worry . . .'

'She'll no listen to ye,' began Macdonald, and looked round to find that Olivia Winter had come into the office. 'Oh, Miss Winter,' he said, 'could ye find the address of Mrs. Isobel Mayne for us?'

'Mrs. Isobel Mayne?' she repeated, looking at him curiously.

'Yes, ye'll find it in one of the old files . . .'

'Mr. Macdonald' — she was hesitant and ill-at-ease — 'Mr. Macdonald . . . excuse me . . . but I couldn't help hearing what Mr. Brett said just now . . . about the Regency Theatre. You — you're not thinking of re-opening it, are you?'

'We're hoping to, Miss Winter, if we can get it.'

'Don't, Mr. Brett,' she said, earnestly, 'don't.'

'Why not?' he demanded in surprise.

'Because it's dangerous,' she said, seriously. 'Evil clings to places and that old building must be steeped in it — evil and violence. Murder has been shut up there for thirty years . . . Don't let it out.

41

Mr. Brett, don't let it out. If you do — what happened once may happen again.'

Macdonald was the first to recover after this astonishing outburst.

'What do you mean, Miss Winter?' he snapped. 'Have ye taken leave of your senses?'

'I'm sorry, Mr. Macdonald.' Once more she was the impersonal secretary. 'You wanted the address of Mrs. Isobel Mayne?' She was turning towards the door when Brett stopped her.

'Do you really believe what you said just now?' he asked.

'Yes, Mr. Brett,' she answered.

'Why?'

'Thoughts and emotions — evil thoughts and emotions attach themselves to places. The Regency Theatre is a haunted building . . .'

'Rubbish!' growled Macdonald.

'It's not — really it's not . . . These things are *real* . . .'

'Do you mean,' put in Keith, 'that because a murder was committed in the Regency Theatre thirty years ago there's

42

danger of the same thing happening again?'

'Not the *same* thing.' She looked at him steadily. 'Thought is a living thing — it cannot be destroyed. It is the thought behind that thirty-year-old murder — the will to kill — that still lives and is chained to the place of its inception . . . '

'Cor lumme — yer givin' me the creeps,' said Nutty.

'But these thoughts can have no power,' said Brett. 'They can't be dangerous . . . '

'You think not?' She raised her eyebrows slightly.

'Of course not — how can they?'

'Thought is all powerful. It goes on and on and it attracts other and similar thoughts to it . . . '

'I'm surprised at ye, Miss Winter,' broke in Macdonald impatiently. 'I always thought ye were a sane an' practical woman . . . '

'I'm both sane and practical, Mr. Macdonald,' retorted Olivia. 'We are all entitled to our own opinions and I have made a study of the subject. I say that if

43

you re-open the Regency Theatre you will be running a very great risk.' She opened the door and paused with the handle in her hand. 'You will be letting loose something that is better left shut up,' she said seriously, and went out, shutting the door behind her.

'Weel,' muttered Macdonald, rubbing his bald head, 'I'd never have believed it . . . never.'

'I couldn't make 'ead nor tail of it,' said Potts. 'Wot's she gettin' at?'

'I've read of such things,' said Ronnie Hays. 'Some people say that the simulacra of certain highly emotional events — such as murder or suicide — still continue to take place on the spot where they were originally enacted. That, I believe, is one of the accepted explanations for ghosts.'

'I think it's a lot of balderdash,' declared Brett.

'Aye, I agree with ye . . . '

'How long will she be finding that address?'

'It shouldna take her long, Brett. It's in one of the old files with some letters from Castleton Mayne aboot casting . . . '

44

'Good heavens, Mac,' said Keith with a grin, 'you weren't a theatrical agent as far back as that, surely?'

'I took over a lot of stuff from my predecessor,' answered Macdonald.

Clifford Brett took out his case and helped himself to a cigarette.

'Ghosts or no ghosts,' he said, 'we're going to re-open the Regency Theatre. I'd like to see Phillip Defoe's face when the bills go up . . .'

'And Madeleine Peters', too,' said Keith.

* * *

The street was one of those drab ones which abound in Pimlico. On either side tall stucco-fronted houses, almost grey from an accumulation of fog and soot, rose up to the dun-coloured sky; ugly buildings with steps that led up to pillared porches and basements guarded by iron railings.

Angus Macdonald stopped the taxi before one of these, as like the rest as one pin in a row, opened the door and got

45

out. Brett followed, standing on the pavement and staring up at the front door.

'This is the house?' he asked.

'Aye,' answered Macdonald, joining him after paying the cabman. 'This is where the Maynes live.'

'Ugly-looking place, isn't it?' grunted Brett.

'These old Victorian houses always look drear and drab,' said Macdonald. 'It was an ugly period . . . Ye know, I'm thinkin' we'll only be wasting our time . . . '

'Well, we'll see . . . ' Clifford Brett led the way up the steps and searched for the bell. It was an old-fashioned iron bell-pull and they heard the jangling din it set up inside the house.

'The old lady is goin' to take a power of convincing,' remarked Macdonald as they waited. 'She's over seventy, ye know, an' no so guid in the head.'

'We've got to convince her,' said Brett.

Footsteps came faintly from behind the closed door and it was opened by a small, white-haired little woman, dressed in black, with a rosy face that was like a wrinkled apple.

'Yes?' she said in a shrill, cockney voice. 'What is it you want?'

'Is Mrs. Mayne at home?' asked Brett.

'That depends what yer want?' she answered shortly.

'Do ye no remember me, Mrs. Duppy?' asked Macdonald.

The little woman thrust out her head and peered up at him with twinkling blue eyes.

'Can't say as I do . . . ' she began.

'Come noo,' interrupted Macdonald, 'ye surely remember Angus Macdonald? I was stage manager at the Coronet Theatre . . . '

'Why, of course!' The faded blue eyes lit up. 'It's a good few years ago since them days. I went to the Coronet as wardrobe mistress just after the Regency was closed . . . '

'Aye, ye were Isobel Mayne's dresser, were ye not?'

'That's right.' Her little pink face clouded. 'Poor thing — she was different then . . . Come inside, we can't stand talking on the step . . . '

She opened the door wider and they entered the hall.

'Do you think we could see Mrs. Mayne?' asked Brett.

'Well, I don't know,' said the little woman doubtfully. 'She's — she's a bit daft, you know, and sometimes . . . What did you want with her?'

Before either could answer there came a voice from the head of the stair — a deep voice with a musical cadence that was only slightly blurred with age.

'Who are you talking to, Duppy?'

The little woman turned and looked up the dark stairs. There was nobody in sight.

'Two gentlemen have called to see you, dearie,' she called.

'To see me?' There was surprise in the tone. 'Good gracious, who are they? What do they want?'

'If we can see you for a few minutes, Mrs. Mayne,' said Brett, 'I'll explain . . . '

'Of course — of course you can see me. Duppy — bring them up — bring them up . . . ' They heard the sound of a stick tapping across the landing above, followed by the opening of a door.

'You're lucky,' whispered the woman called Duppy, 'she's in one of her good moods. This way.'

She led the way up the staircase. There were a great number of pictures on the walls, and when they reached the landing they saw, under a long window, a tall palm stand. The whole house was like something out of another era. There were two doors opening off the wide landing, and the little woman crossed to one of these, tapped, and opened it.

'Come in,' called the deep voice that had spoken from the top of the stairs. 'I don't often receive visitors these days.'

They entered a large, lofty room that was furnished in keeping with the rest of the house. Heavy plush curtains hung at the two long windows and there were a great number of spindle-leg tables full of photographs and bric-a-brac. Standing before the fire-place with its draped and fringed mantelshelf was a tall woman with almost snow-white hair. She was dressed in black, and her pale face still retained traces of the beauty that time and age were slowly destroying. She stood regally upright, supporting herself on an ebony stick in one thin, blue-veined hand. She looked at them steadily with eyes that had sunk into a mass of wrinkles.

'I don't think I know you, do I?' she asked.

'I'm Clifford Brett . . . this is Mr. Angus Macdonald.'

'Please sit down,' she said with a slight inclination of the head. 'My son and I were just going to have tea. You would like to join us?'

'Thank you, that's very kind of you, Mrs. Mayne,' said Brett.

'Will you bring the tea, Duppy?' said Mrs. Mayne, 'and tell Mr. Alexander that we have visitors . . . '

'Yes, dearie.' The little, rosy-cheeked woman nodded brightly and withdrew. Mrs. Mayne sat down carefully and with some little difficulty in a big chair by the fire. 'What brings you to see me?' she inquired.

'Well,' answered Brett, 'we're producing a new show . . . '

'Oh, are you in the profession?' she

interrupted quickly, her eyes lighting up. 'I used to be. You wouldn't think to look at me now that I've played Juliet, would you? Juliet . . . and now I cannot walk properly without my stick — 'the staff of my age, my very prop' . . . '

She stopped as the door behind them opened.

'Ah . . . here is my son,' she said. 'Alexander . . . this is Mr. Brett and Mr. Macdonald . . . '

'How do you do?' The newcomer came over to the fire. He was a thin man with stooping shoulders. There was about him an air of weariness as though he found life too tiring. His thinning hair was dark with a touch of grey at the sides and he wore it carefully brushed to hide its scantiness. There was a nervous twitching of his mouth as he looked from one to the other.

'Wasn't it nice of them to come and see me, Alexander?' said his mother. 'So few people come now and yet I remember . . . ' she broke off. 'Alexander was never interested in the stage, were you?'

'No, Mother.'

'He preferred a business career,' she went on. 'Alexander is quite clever at business . . .'

'But not quite clever enough, I'm afraid,' he said. There was bitterness in the tone and in the twist of the mouth. This man, thought Brett, was unhappy. Things had gone wrong for him somewhere and he was resentful.

'You mustn't say that, dear,' said Mrs. Mayne, soothingly. 'You have just been unlucky, that's all . . . Why did you come to see me?' she changed the subject abruptly. 'You were going to tell me . . .'

'We're producing a new revue,' explained Brett. 'We came to see you with a proposition . . .'

'A proposition — *me?*' There was pleasure in the lined face. 'Oh, but I've given up the stage long ago . . .'

'I'm afraid you misunderstand me, Mrs. Mayne,' interrupted Brett. 'We've been let down over a theatre. We want to know if you would consider letting us have the Regency . . . ?'

'*The Regency?*' Her face changed

suddenly and her voice sank to a whisper.

'Yes — we want to re-open it.'

'You . . . you want to . . . *re-open* . . . the Regency?' There was horror in the voice now — fear in the faded eyes.

'We'd make ye a verra good offer,' began Macdonald.

'No — no!' she almost screamed at him. 'No. Alexander . . . send them away — send them away!'

'Mother . . . '

'Send them away,' she cried, 'send them away. I won't listen. I won't listen . . . '

'Mrs. Mayne . . . please . . . ' Brett adopted a conciliatory tone, but she only made an impatient gesture.

'Go away,' she said, 'go away! Alexander, send them away . . . '

'Mother, don't upset yourself . . . '

The door opened and Mrs. Duppy came in carrying a laden tea-tray. Mrs. Mayne turned her head towards her.

'Duppy,' she said pleadingly, 'Duppy — you can make them go away. Make them go away, Duppy . . . '

'What's the matter, dearie — What's the matter?' said the old woman, putting down the tray and coming over to her mistress. 'You're trembling . . . '

'They want to re-open the Regency Theatre, Duppy,' said Mrs. Mayne, 'but they shan't . . . I won't let them . . . *The danger must not come again* . . . '

# 4

Alexander Mayne looked at his mother and his rather weak face was troubled. He coughed, cleared his throat, and fingered his chin nervously.

'Mother, listen to me a minute,' he said. 'Let's be sensible about this . . . Why shouldn't the Regency Theatre be re-opened?'

'You don't understand,' she answered. 'It would be — like opening your father's grave . . . '

'Nonsense,' he exclaimed, impatiently. 'If these gentlemen have a reasonable proposition to make I'm prepared to consider it. We need money urgently . . . It would be foolish to . . . '

'I won't consent to anything of the kind,' she declared, stubbornly.

'I hold your power of attorney,' interrupted Mayne, 'I can agree without your consent . . . '

'You wouldn't,' she whispered. 'You

don't know what you would be doing!'

'Why shouldn't we make a little money out of the place, if we can?' he argued, reasonably. 'It's been a liability to us ever since I can remember . . .'

'You leave it to Mr. Alexander, dearie,' put in Mrs. Duppy, soothingly. 'I'm sure he knows best what to do . . .'

'He doesn't understand,' muttered Mrs. Mayne, shaking her head. 'There's danger there — danger!'

'Oh, come now, Mrs. Mayne,' said Brett. 'How can there be any danger?'

'My husband was killed there, Mr. Brett,' she answered. '*They* murdered him . . . The evil forces are still active, waiting — waiting for another chance . . .'

'We'd be prepared to risk it,' said Brett with a smile.

Her eyes flashed angrily, and a faint flush stained the pale cheeks.

'You don't believe me?' she said. 'You think these are only the foolish fancies of an old woman. You're wrong! The danger is real. Leave the Regency Theatre alone . . . There is death there . . .'

'Mother, do try and be sensible,' urged

Mayne. 'Because Father was killed there thirty years ago . . . '

'The evil has not dispersed, Alexander. It is only — dormant.'

'I'm sure there's nothing there to harm anyone, Mother . . . '

She struck her hand on the arm of her chair in sudden passion.

'Oh, why are you so blind?' she cried. 'Why can't I make you understand? You mustn't do this — you mustn't!'

'We understand how ye feel about it, Mrs. Mayne,' broke in Angus Macdonald. 'The Regency holds tragic memories for ye. But ye must realize that it's doing no good to anybody as it is. Surely it would be better, as your son says, to make some profit out of it . . . ?'

'Of course it would,' agreed Mayne. 'Don't you see that, Mother?'

'You will never get me to agree,' said Mrs. Mayne, shaking her head. 'If you do this thing — as you say you can, without my consent, you will be solely responsible for what happens. You can never say I didn't warn you . . . '

'I'm only doing what I think is for the

best,' said Mayne, a little uneasily.

'I'm quite sure nothing *will* happen,' said Brett. 'If you could only bring yourself to see . . . '

'I would rather have nothing more to do with the matter,' she interrupted, 'except to say this: my husband's dressing room is locked and the door sealed — I sealed it myself when the theatre was shut thirty years ago. I will not have it disturbed, you understand, Alexander? It must not be opened — the seals must remain unbroken . . . '

'We would be willing to agree to that,' said Brett, quickly.

'If you do this monstrous thing, Alexander,' continued Mrs. Mayne, ignoring the interruption, 'you will see that this is made conditional. You promise me?'

He nodded reluctantly.

'Very well, Mother . . . '

With difficulty Mrs. Mayne got up.

'Help me to my room, Duppy,' she said. 'I am going to lie down for a little while.'

'What about yer tea, dearie?' asked the old woman.

'I don't want any.'

'I'll bring you a nice hot cup to yer room, shall I?'

'No, I would rather be left alone.' Slowly, with the assistance of Mrs. Duppy, she walked to the door. On the threshold, she turned.

'Change your mind, Alexander,' she said in a broken voice. 'Change your mind before it is too late. Nothing but disaster can come of it . . . disaster, and possibly — death.'

She looked at them for a moment, and then, turning, went out. They heard the tap-tap of her stick on the landing, the opening and shutting of a door, and then — silence.

Alexander Mayne was the first to speak. He cleared his throat, fiddling with his tie.

'You must — forgive my mother,' he said, jerkily. 'She's — she's — well, a little eccentric . . .'

'I'm sorry that we should have distressed her,' said Brett.

'I feel rather — unhappy — about it,' muttered Mayne, thrusting his hands into his pockets and gently teetering on his toes. 'But I'm sure I'm doing the sensible thing . . . for both of us.'

'I'm quite sure of that,' said Brett.

'I think ye'll find she'll become reconciled when she finds nothing very dreadful happens,' remarked Macdonald.

'That's what I'm hoping.' Alexander Mayne nodded. 'And, of course, nothing will . . .'

'I wouldn't be too sure of that, Mr. Alexander.' Mrs. Duppy had come quietly in and was stooping over the tray. 'You might be wrong . . .'

★ ★ ★

Keith Gilbert sat at the piano in the living room of the flat he shared with Ronnie Hays and played snatches of melody. On the music rack in front of him was a sheet of music paper covered with pencilled notes. He played a few bars, altered the tune slightly, played it again and jotted down the result on the paper before him. It was so full of erasures and additions that nobody except the composer could have hoped to understand it. Presently, with a grunt of satisfaction, he sat back on the piano stool.

'Ronnie!' he called.

'What do you want?' asked Hays from the other room.

'Come here a minute,' shouted Keith, and when the other appeared in the doorway: 'How do you like this?'

He played and sang the number he had been composing, and Ronnie Hays listened critically. It was a tuneful number with a lilting lyric — catchy and easily remembered. When he came to the end he swung round on the stool and looked at his friend.

'Like it?' he asked.

'Very much,' said Hays.

'I hope Clifford'll like it,' said Keith. 'I think it's what he wanted for that scene in the second half . . . '

'I wonder how he's getting on at the Maynes' said Hays.

'He said he'd come along here, or telephone, when he had any news, didn't he?'

'Yes — I hope the deuce he'll pull it off.'

'So do I.' Keith made a grimace. 'We're sunk if he doesn't.'

'That was a *filthy* trick of Defoe's,' said Hays, frowning.

'Tangye warned us what he was like, didn't she?'

'She's a nice kid, you know,' said Hays, 'clever, too . . . '

'Too clever to be in the chorus,' said Keith. 'I'm going to speak to Clifford about her . . . What are you looking for?'

'Cigarettes . . . '

'They're on the top of the piano — under that music . . . '

Hays found the box and helped himself to a cigarette. Just as he was searching for his lighter the front doorbell rang.

'I'll bet that's Clifford,' he exclaimed as he went to the door.

'Keep your fingers crossed,' called Keith after him.

But it wasn't Brett. When he opened the door he found Tangye there.

'I came to see if there was any news,' she explained.

'Come in,' said Hays. He shut the door and led her into the sitting room.

'Hello, Tangye.' Keith got up from the piano. 'Sit down.' He pushed forward a chair. 'Have a cigarette?'

She took one from the box he held out and Hays lit it for her.

'Thank you,' she said. 'Have you heard anything from Mr. Brett yet?'

'No,' answered Keith. 'We thought it was Clifford when you rang.'

'He's taking a long time,' said Hays. 'That looks promising. If they'd turned him down flat we should have heard by now . . . '

The telephone bell interrupted the end of the sentence.

'That must be Clifford now,' he said.

'I'll take it,' said Keith, quickly. 'Excuse me, Tangye . . . '

He went over to the instrument and lifted the receiver. The nasal voice of Nutty Potts came over the wire. He was in a call-box he said — at Tottenham Court Road — was there any news? Gilbert told him they hadn't heard anything yet, and Nutty said all right, he'd come round.

'It was Nutty,' said Keith as he put the receiver back on the rack. 'He's coming round.'

'I *do* hope it will be all right,' said Tangye.

'It's got to be,' answered Ronnie Hays. 'It 'ud be just too bad if we had to pack up the show now.'

'We're not going to pack it up,' said Keith. 'The show's going on, and Defoe and Madeleine Peters are going to gnash their teeth with rage every time they see the 'house full' boards outside the Regency Theatre.'

They laughed.

'I would like to know why Defoe changed his mind about letting you have the Rialto,' remarked Tangye thoughtfully, after a pause.

'Because Madeleine Peters walked out,' said Keith.

'That's what he said,' said Tangye, doubtfully, 'but do you think that was the real reason?'

'What other could he have?' asked Hays.

'I don't know' — she shook her head — 'but I can't imagine Defoe doing anything unless he was going to gain by it . . .'

'Madeleine Peters made him do this — just for spite,' declared Keith with conviction. 'She's got him completely under her thumb.'

'Perhaps,' murmured Tangye, but she didn't sound very convinced. They began chatting about the show and Keith played over the new number. Just as he finished the doorbell rang again. It was Nutty. He came in with a grin on his rugged face.

''Ullo,' he greeted, ''eard anythink yet?'

'Not a thing,' said Keith.

The little man screwed up his face.

'Cor lumme,' he grunted, 'they're a long time, aren't they? Wotcher think the chances are, eh?'

'No news is good news, Nutty,' said Hays.

'So they say, don't they?' grinned Nutty. 'Well, let's 'ope it's right in this case. 'Ere, you know that blinkin' girl Maysie — Maysie Sheringham?'

'Have you been chasing her *again?*'

asked Keith, laughing.

'Chasin' 'er?' echoed Nutty. 'Lumme, yer got a fine chance o' doin' that — she's gone before yer can blink. I was just thinkin' of 'oppin' in somewhere fer a cupper this afternoon when I suddenly spots 'er in front of a posh 'otel. 'Eres yer chance, Nutty, old cock, I says ter meself, an' up I goes an' asks 'er if she'd like some tea. 'Very much, Mr. Potts,' she says, 'I'm just goin' 'ome ter 'ave some,' an' before yer can blink, she's off.'

They all burst out laughing. The expression on the little man's face was so aggrieved that it was ludicrous.

'Poor old Nutty,' began Hays, and stopped as for the third time the doorbell rang. 'It must be Clifford this time,' he said, and hurried out into the hall. It was Clifford, and they had only to take one look at his face to know the answer to the question they were all concerned about.

'We've got it!' he cried almost before he was across the threshold. 'The agreement will be signed tomorrow morning.'

'Did you have much trouble — getting round Isobel Mayne?' asked Keith.

'We'd never have got the place at all if it had been left to her,' answered Brett. He gave them a brief account of the interview. 'We're getting it for a hundred and fifty a week plus five per cent of the gross box office receipts,' he concluded.

'That seems reasonable,' commented Hays.

'I don't think it's bad,' agreed Brett. 'Of course we shall have to spend a bit in putting it to rights . . . '

'Is it in a very bad state?' asked Keith.

'We've no seen it yet,' said Macdonald. 'The keys are at Mayne's bank, and it was closed, ye see. He's taking us over the theatre tomorrow morning after we've signed the agreement at his lawyer's . . . '

'Isn't that rather like buying a pig in a poke?' said Hays cautiously.

Brett shrugged his shoulders.

'It is in a way,' he answered, 'but beggars can't be choosers. This theatre's our only hope. We've got to take a chance on it. If we'd haggled at all, Mayne might have called the whole thing off . . . '

'Why haven't they let it before?' asked Tangye.

'That's the old lady,' said Brett. 'She's got an idea that the place is dangerous.'

'Dangerous?'

'She thinks there are evil forces lurking there,' Brett grinned. 'All nonsense, of course, but she's a bit cracked . . . '

'She and Olivia Winter ought to get together,' remarked Keith.

'Aye,' said Macdonald. 'They'd make a good pair.'

'When do we see the theatre?' said Hays. 'Tomorrow morning?'

'Yes,' replied Brett. 'You'd better meet us there. We've got to meet Mayne at his lawyer's first. By the way, we had to give Mrs. Mayne one concession . . . '

'Aye,' said Macdonald, nodding, 'she insists that her husband's old dressing room shall remain locked and sealed.'

'What for?' said Ronnie Hays. 'What's the idea of that?'

'Sheer sentiment, I think,' said Brett. 'Apparently she locked and sealed it herself when the theatre was closed. I agreed.'

'It's a queer thing to insist on,' remarked Keith.

'You wouldn't think anything that Isobel Mayne did was queer if you'd met her,' said Brett. 'Maybe she believes her 'evil forces' are locked up there.' He laughed, and then suddenly becoming serious: 'We've still got a problem to solve, you chaps. Who's going to take the place of Madeleine Peters?'

'I've been thinking about that,' said Macdonald, thoughtfully. 'It's no going to be so easy to find anyone. Everybody with a name is working or already under contract . . . '

'Well, we've got to find somebody,' began Brett.

'What about — Tangye?' interrupted Keith Gilbert, quietly.

'Tangye . . . ?'

'But she hasna got a name . . . ' Macdonald sounded dubious.

'Everybody's got ter start sometime, ain't they?' said Nutty. 'I say give 'er a chance.'

'Look, Clifford,' said Keith, persuasively, 'she's good. You saw what she could do when she took Madeleine Peters' place at rehearsal . . . '

69

'Yes, I know.'

'We could give her a big boost of publicity . . . New discovery — all that kind of stuff,' continued Keith.

Brett frowned. He was obviously undecided what to do. After a moment he turned to Tangye.

'What do you say, Tangye?' he said. 'Do you think you could do it?'

'Oh, yes, Mr. Brett.' She sounded breathless, as though she had been running. 'I'm sure I could . . . '

'Course yer could,' said Nutty. 'Let 'er 'ave a bash . . . '

'What do you think, Ronnie?' asked Brett.

'I think it's a very good idea,' answered Hays without hesitation.

'All right,' Brett nodded. 'That's fixed. Come along to the office tomorrow, Tangye, and we'll give you a contract.'

She looked at him with shining eyes.

'Do you really mean it?' she said.

'Yes, of course.'

'But . . . Oh, it's wonderful . . . I — I don't know what to say . . . ' The brightness in her eyes was in danger of overflowing. Keith saw the tears gathering and hastily held out a box of cigarettes.

'Don't say anything,' he advised. 'Have a cigarette?'

'Thank you,' she said, unsteadily. 'I won't let you down. I — I promise . . . '

Before they could reply the doorbell rang. It rang twice — quickly — urgently.

'Who the dickens is that?' muttered Hays as he hurried into the hall. They heard him open the front door. There was a pause and then a startled exclamation.

'I say,' he called excitedly. 'Come here, all of you . . . '

They went out into the hall and joined him at the open front door.

'What's the matter — ?' began Brett.

'Look at that — on the panel of the door,' said Hays, pointing.

They looked. On the white paint had been scrawled words — words in a bright, glistening scarlet that stood out vividly.

'It's been written in grease paint,' said Tangye, wonderingly.

'*Keep away from the Regency Theatre.*' Brett read out the message slowly.

'*There is death there.*'

'Blimey!' breathed Nutty Potts. 'Who coulda done that?'

'It's queer handwriting,' said Keith.

'Aye,' agreed Macdonald, and there was a strange edge to his voice. 'Verra queer. It's the handwriting of a dead man!'

Tangye uttered a little gasp, and the others turned to him with surprised faces.

'A — a *dead* man . . . ?' Brett was beginning incredulously, when Macdonald interrupted him.

'Aye,' he said, seriously. 'That is the handwriting of Castleton Mayne!'

# 5

The head waiter bowed deferentially.

'Everything to your satisfaction, Mr, Defoe?' he asked.

'Yes, thank you, Charles,' said Phillip Defoe. 'You can bring another bottle of champagne.'

'At once.' The head waiter bowed again. 'I'll tell the wine waiter.'

He moved away from the table, and Defoe leaned across to Madeleine Peters.

'Who rang you up and told you that Brett was re-opening the Regency Theatre?' he asked in a low voice.

She shook her head.

'I've told you, Phillip, I don't know,' she said. 'It was a queer voice — a kind of husky whisper. It might have been a man or a woman. You couldn't tell.'

Defoe frowned and played with the stem of his glass.

'I don't understand it,' he muttered. 'Why did this person, whoever it was, think that you would be interested?'

'I've no idea,' she answered. 'If Brett has got this theatre it's going to spoil your little scheme, isn't it?'

'Perhaps.' He pursed his rather thick lips. 'There may be — ways of seeing that it doesn't . . . '

'What's at the back of your mind now?' she asked, quickly.

'They haven't opened at the Regency — yet,' he replied, significantly.

'Well, I don't see what's to stop them, *if* they've got it,' she said. 'It's that old place in Oxford Street, isn't it?'

He waited while the waiter brought another bottle of wine and opened it. When he had filled their glasses and set the bottle in the ice-pail, bowed, and taken his departure, Defoe said:

'That's the place. They call it the haunted theatre.'

'Why?' she demanded. 'Is it haunted?'

He shrugged his shoulders and took a sip of wine.

'That depends on whether you believe in such things. It has the reputation of being queer. Castleton Mayne, the

Shakespearian actor — I don't suppose you've heard of him — was murdered on the stage thirty years ago. That's why the theatre was shut . . . '

'Do you mean . . . his ghost is supposed to haunt the place?' Madeleine looked sceptical.

'So the story goes.' Defoe took a cigar from his case and carefully removed the band. 'People have seen things, I believe . . . '

'What sort of things?'

'Lights at night — voices . . . '

'Voices?'

He pierced the end of the cigar with a gold piercer and lit it deliberately before he replied.

'Yes,' he said, blowing out a cloud of smoke. 'They say it is Mayne — re-enacting some of the scenes that made him famous . . . '

'What nonsense!' she laughed.

'Very possibly,' he agreed, looking at her through the blue smoke. 'People imagine things easily.'

Madeleine drank some champagne. Her eyes were thoughtful. She set the glass down and after a pause said:

'Phillip . . . ?'

He was looking at her with a little smile playing about his mouth.

'Yes?' he said softly. 'Go on, Madeleine . . . '

'Supposing,' she began, and stopped. 'Wait — let me think . . . '

'Shall I tell you what you are thinking, my dear?' he inquired. 'You are wondering if we could not use this — this legend of the Regency Theatre to our advantage . . . Is that right?'

'Yes,' she answered. 'How did you know?'

'Because,' he replied, 'I am thinking exactly the same thing.'

★ ★ ★

The Regency Theatre occupies a site near the lower end of Oxford Street. Its once attractive, if rather ornate, façade is drab and grimed with the accumulated dirt and smoke of years; its doors are boarded up and the frames which once held gay bills and photographs are glassless. The canopy over the entrance is broken and the sockets where once lights blazed are rusted and useless. Like something long dead it stands sightless, mouldering away to dust, and forgotten by the crowds which hurry past it every day.

A taxi drew into the kerb in front of this dilapidated building and Clifford Brett and Angus Macdonald got out. Brett dropped some coins into the driver's outstretched palm.

'Thank yer, sir,' said the old man, stowing them away beneath his voluminous clothing. 'Seems funny bein' asked ter take anyone ter the Regency these days. I can remember drivin' 'em 'ere night arter night . . . '

'I hope you will again,' said Brett.

'Why — is it bein' re-opened?' asked the driver, as he put up his flag.

'I hope so. My friends and I are thinking of taking it and putting on a new show . . . '

'Well, good luck ter yer,' said the cabman. 'Seems all wrong some'ow ter see it all boarded up an' dirty when yer can remember what it *was* like . . . '

He drove away and they stood on the pavement looking about them.

'The stage door will be up the side-turning, I'm thinkin',' remarked Macdonald. He led the way up a narrow passage. 'Mayne should be here, it's just twelve-thirty . . . '

'There's Keith and Ronnie, anyway,' said Brett.

They were standing in front of a partly open door set in the high brick wall that formed one side of the passageway.

'Hello, Clifford,' greeted Keith. 'Everything all right?'

'Yes, the contract is all signed, sealed and delivered,' answered Brett.

'Good,' said Keith. 'Mayne's here.'

'Have you seen him?' asked Brett.

'No.' Keith shook his head. 'I wouldn't know him if I did. But the stage door's open, so I presume he must be inside . . . '

'Here's Tangye,' interrupted Hays.

The girl came up to them quickly.

'I was afraid I'd be late,' she said, breathlessly. 'I couldn't get a taxi.'

'We've only just got here,' said Brett.

'Where's Nutty? Have you seen . . . '

''Mornin' all.' Nutty's voice broke in as he appeared from the dark interior of the theatre. 'The door was open when I got 'ere, so I popped inside fer a dekko . . . '

'Did ye no see Mr. Mayne?' asked Macdonald.

'I ain't seen nobody . . . '

'Why didn't he come with you and Macdonald?' said Hays.

'He had to go to the bank and collect the keys,' explained Brett. 'He must be inside somewhere. Let's go and find him.'

They went over to the narrow door and squeezed through. It was very dark inside, but as their eyes became accustomed to it they were able to see dimly. Just inside the stage door there was a sort of cubby hole — the stage doorkeeper's box. It was still lined with faded and dusty photographs, and on a shelf was an old-fashioned telephone. On the wall opposite was a board covered with tattered green baize, to which were still pinned yellow and faded notices. A gas jet, enclosed in a wire cage, stuck out beside it. Beyond was a passage leading to absolute blackness.

There was a smell of old canvas and size, grease paint and perfume, mingled with damp and dust — the smell peculiar to all theatres.

'The light's turned off at the main, I suppose,' said Brett, pressing a switch and finding that nothing happened.

Tangye shivered.

'It's a bit chilly, isn't it?' she said.

'Bit niffy, too,' remarked Nutty, sniffing.

They felt their way to the end of the passage.

'Mayne must be here somewhere,' grunted Brett.

'Gone through to the stage, I expect,' said Macdonald. 'I wish there was some light here . . . '

'Mind, there's a bend here,' called Keith from a little way in front. 'Hold on — I'll strike a match.'

There was the scrape of a match against the box and then a tiny flame flickered in the darkness. By its light they saw that the passage had widened. Doors opened on one side, several of them.

'There are the dressing rooms,' said Brett. He looked at one with a heavily barred door. 'That's Castleton Mayne's, I suppose?'

'Aye,' said Macdonald, nodding. 'Ye can see the seals the old lady was talking about.'

'I haven't felt any evil forces yet, have you?' asked Brett.

At that moment the match went out and Tangye gave a frightened gasp.

'I'll strike another,' said Keith. 'Did you think a ghostly breath had blown it out, Tangye?'

'No, but it's a little — eerie,' she answered.

Again the light nickered as Keith struck another match.

'There's the door to the stage,' said Brett. He pointed to an iron door at the top of some steps. Macdonald went over, mounted the steps, and pushed against the door. It opened slowly, creaking loudly on rusty hinges. They followed him through on to the stage of the Regency Theatre. There was more light here. It came through the dusty windows at the back of the circle, small squares like postage stamps in the cavern of gloom that formed the great auditorium.

'It's bigger than I expected,' remarked Brett, looking round. His voice echoed hollowly. 'We shan't have to alter the scenery much.'

'It's quite a big place altogether,' said Macdonald. 'I wonder where the deuce Mayne can be?'

'He must be somewhere about,' said Brett. 'He must have opened the stage door.' He raised his voice and shouted. 'Mr. Mayne! Mr. Mayne!'

Only the echoes answered him. There was no sound or movement in the empty theatre.

'He's not here,' muttered Hays. 'He must have heard *that*.'

'Queer,' remarked Macdonald, 'maybe he went out for something . . . '

'Lumme, look at the dust,' said Nutty. 'Like a blinkin' army blanket, ain't it?'

'Yes,' said Keith, and then suddenly: 'I say — look over there!'

'What is it?' Tangye's voice was shrill and startled.

'Somebody's been using a broom,' said Keith.

'Oh,' she said in relief. 'You frightened me. I wondered what you'd seen . . . '

'It must have been Mayne,' began Brett. 'Nobody else . . . '

'Listen,' broke in Hays. 'Can you hear anything?'

They stood quite still. Somewhere quite near they could hear a faint sound like the dripping of water.

'Leaking pipe somewhere,' said Brett.

'It seems to be up in the 'grid',' said Keith, looking up at the 'flies' where the backcloths and borders and the tangle of ropes that hoisted the scenery could be dimly seen in the gloom.

They stood quite still. Somewhere quite near they could hear a faint sound like the dripping of water.

And then Tangye screamed!

'It's *blood*!' she cried hysterically. 'Look . . . look . . . on my hand . . . '

They crowded round her

'It can't be . . . ' muttered Brett.

'It is,' she declared tearfully, staring in horror at the stain on the back of her hand. 'It *is* blood . . . '

There was a sound from above them — a queer slithering sound. Something came down out of the darkness and fell with a horrid thud on the dusty boards of the stage. Tangye screamed again.

'What was it?' she whispered. 'What was it — '

'My God!' Clifford Brett was bending over the thing that sprawled at his feet. 'It's Mayne — Alexander Mayne . . . '

'Aye, it's Mayne,' said Macdonald, soberly. 'Look at his throat . . . '

# 6

They stared down at the thing at their feet that sprawled so horribly in the grey dust, and Keith Gilbert was the first to find his voice.

'Do . . . do you think it was suicide?' he asked, huskily.

'I don't know,' whispered Brett. 'There's a wound in his throat . . . it's cut through one of the arteries . . .'

'Is he dead?' asked Ronnie Hays.

'Yes, nobody could live very long after a wound like that,' answered Brett.

'Castleton Mayne died from a stab in the throat,' muttered Macdonald.

'Now don't start suggesting . . .' began Brett, and was interrupted by a little gulping sound from Tangye. 'What's the matter?' he asked, quickly.

'Please, would you . . . would you mind if I . . . went outside?' Her voice was shaky, and in the dim light she looked curiously green.

'Take her away, one of you,' said Brett. 'Take her out and give her some coffee or something . . . '

'I'll take her,' said Keith. 'Come along, Tangye . . . '

He took her by the arm and she looked up at him with a wry smile.

'I'm sorry to be so . . . silly,' she murmured.

'What you want is a double brandy, my girl,' said Keith. 'Come along.'

He led her away from the horror in the dust, and through the iron door at the back of the stage.

'I thought she was going to faint, poor kid,' said Brett.

'Aye, it must have been a nasty shock for her,' said Macdonald.

'It was a nasty shock for all of us,' remarked Hays. 'Where did he fall from?'

'The 'catwalk',' answered Brett, looking up into the shadowy world of hanging ropes and canvases above.

'What's the 'catwalk'?' demanded Nutty.

'A narrow gangway up in the 'grid',' answered Brett. 'The stage hands and electricians use it.'

'What on earth was he doing up there?' asked Hays, pursing his lips in a puzzled way.

'God knows,' said Brett, shaking his head. 'He must have died there . . . '

'I canna see any sort of weapon,' remarked Macdonald, looking about the dusty stage.

'It probably dropped out of his hand when he — when he killed himself,' said Hays.

'*If* he killed himself,' said Macdonald, significantly.

They looked at him. He had put into words the thought that had been in the back of all their minds . . . that this was murder.

'If there's no knife or something of the kind here, it canna be anything but murder,' went on Macdonald.

'We can soon settle that,' said Brett. 'If there's a weapon anywhere it will be up on the 'catwalk' . . . '

'I'll nip up an' 'ave a look,' volunteered Nutty. ''Ow d'yer get up there?'

Brett showed him the narrow iron

ladder at the side of the stage.

'O.K.,' said Nutty. 'I won't be a tick.'

He went over to the ladder and began to climb up into the shadows.

'If it *is* murder,' muttered Brett, 'who could have done it — and why?'

'Do ye mind what Isobel Mayne said?' asked Macdonald seriously, 'about there being danger and — death . . . '

'Coincidence,' retorted Brett, emphatically. 'It can't be anything else. She couldn't have *known* this was going to happen . . . '

'What about that message, Clifford, scrawled on our front door?' said Hays.

'In Castleton Mayne's handwriting,' put in Macdonald.

'It must have been a fake,' said Brett. 'The man's been dead for thirty years. It's ridiculous to suppose that . . . '

He broke off as Nutty's voice called down from above.

'There ain't no sign of a knife up 'ere . . . '

'Are you quite sure, Nutty?'

'Yes . . . there's a lot o' blood 'ere, but nothink else . . . '

'Then it must have been murder,' said Macdonald.

'It certainly looks like it,' agreed Brett. 'Can you see any marks in the dust, Nutty? Footprints or anything?'

'It's a funny thing, yer know,' answered Nutty in a puzzled tone, 'but there ain't no dust up 'ere . . . '

'No dust? But the place is thick with it . . . '

'Not up 'ere it ain't,' declared Nutty. 'It's been swep' clean.'

'All right, Nutty, come down,' said Brett. He looked at the others. 'That doesn't leave much doubt. Mayne couldn't have swept the place. The murderer did that to wipe out his tracks.'

'When?' asked Macdonald quickly. 'There couldna have been much time. Mayne couldna have been here very long before we arrived . . . '

'There must have been time enough,' said Brett, with a glance at the body. 'It washes out the supernatural, anyway. You can't imagine a ghost with a broom.'

'I say,' remarked Hays, suddenly. 'If Mayne was dead — up there — when we arrived, what made him fall when he did?'

'Some kind of muscular spasm, I should think,' said Brett. 'The body was precariously balanced, and when Tangye screamed . . . '

He was interrupted by the return of Nutty Potts.

'Blimey, it's no cake walk up there,' said the little man, with a grin. 'The place where 'e fell from's only about a foot an' a 'alf wide, with a bit o' railin' ter keep yer from tumblin' over. The place is swimmin' with blood . . . '

'Look here,' broke in Macdonald, 'we oughtn't to be talking. We should do something. This is serious . . . '

'Yes, you're right,' agreed Brett. 'We'd better inform the police. I'll . . . '

'Sh-s-s,' muttered Hays. 'Listen . . . '

They listened, almost holding their breaths. And then they heard it. The faint sound of a tapping stick. It came from beyond the iron door and was drawing slowly nearer.

'Somebody's coming along the passage from the stage door,' whispered Brett, and even as he finished the sentence a voice called faintly:

'Alexander . . . Alexander . . . Are you there, Alexander?'

'It's Isobel Mayne,' breathed Brett.

'Keep her away, Brett,' said Macdonald, urgently. 'You must keep her away . . . The shock might be dangerous . . . '

'I'll try,' answered Brett. He went over to the door, pulled it open, and called: 'Is that you, Mrs. Mayne?'

'Who is that?' she answered, sharply.

'Clifford Brett. Don't come any farther, Mrs. Mayne. It's very dark . . . You might fall over something . . . '

She was standing at the foot of the steps, her white face very clear in the shadows.

'Is my son with you?' she asked.

'No, no, he's not,' said Brett, quickly.

'Are you sure?' There was doubt in the still resonant voice.

'Yes . . . yes, of course,' he answered. 'You shouldn't have come here, Mrs. Mayne . . . '

'Why not?' she said. 'The Regency is

91

familiar ground to me ... Where is Alexander?'

'Don't you think you ought to go home?' he urged. 'Let me put you in a taxi ... '

'What are you trying to keep from me?' she demanded, suspiciously.

'Nothing,' he began, but she interrupted him.

'You are. I can feel that you are.' She began to mount the stone steps slowly. 'You are trying to hide something. What has happened — tell me?'

'Mrs. Mayne,' said Brett, 'please don't come any farther ... '

She took no notice. With difficulty she climbed the steps and pushed him to one side.

'Who are those people on the stage?' she asked, peering past him.

'Only friends of mine,' he said. 'Please, Mrs. Mayne ... '

She ignored him. Slowly, hesitantly, she advanced across the bare stage. They watched her in silence. There was nothing they could do to stop her except by using force. Macdonald took a step forward.

'Stop her, Brett — ye must stop her,' he said.

She pushed him out of the way.

'Let me pass,' she said, firmly.

At last she reached the spot where Mayne lay. She stopped, looking down at what remained of her son. They heard her quick, indrawn breath. It whistled dryly in her throat.

'His father died there,' she said. 'If you brush away the dust you will find an older stain . . . '

'Come away,' said Brett, gently. 'You'll only upset yourself . . . '

She shook off the hand he had laid on her arm.

'I warned you what would happen if you re-opened this place,' she said. 'I told Alexander, but he would not listen . . . '

'How could ye possibly know?' said Macdonald.

'It happened before,' she replied. 'There is evil here. The air is thick with it. Can't you feel it?'

'Mrs. Mayne,' began Brett uneasily, but she went on as though he had not spoken.

'You must be convinced *now* that what

I said was true. Doesn't *that* prove it?' She pointed at the body of Alexander Mayne. 'Oh, why don't you go? Yesterday my son was alive and well. If he had never set foot within this accursed building he would still be so. There is danger here. It lurks in every shadow — in every brick and stone. Leave this place' — she flung out her arms and her voice rose shrilly — 'leave it! Death has come twice — if you don't heed what I say it will come again.'

In spite of his scepticism Brett felt his flesh creep. The resonant voice that had thirty years ago filled this old theatre was filling it again. The echoes of it went resounding through the vast space of the auditorium and, as in that bygone day Isobel Mayne had stirred her audience, so she stirred them now.

And then, suddenly, the spell was broken.

Mrs. Duppy's voice, anxious and worried, called from the passage:

'Mrs. Mayne . . . Are yer there, dearie?'

'Duppy . . . Duppy . . . ' The voice was the voice of an old woman now.

94

There was a tremor in it and the hint of a sob.

Mrs. Duppy came hurriedly through the iron door, stumbling in her eagerness.

'I'm coming, dearie,' she panted. 'I'm coming.'

Mrs. Mayne took an uncertain step towards her and the old woman put her arms round her.

'What did you want to come *here* for, dearie?' she said, soothingly. 'I saw you slip out and I followed you . . . ' She stopped with a sudden gasp as she caught sight of the motionless form beyond her mistress. 'Lord save us,' she whispered in horror, 'what's happened?'

'Alexander's dead,' whimpered Mrs. Mayne, burying her face in the other's shoulder. 'My son's dead . . . '

'*Dead?*' Mrs. Duppy's eyes went round with a sort of fearful surprise.

'They killed him — the evil things in this place,' sobbed Isobel Mayne. 'They killed him — as they killed his father . . . '

'Can ye no get her away, Mrs. Duppy?' said Macdonald.

The old woman nodded over Mrs.

Mayne's bowed head.

'You come with me, dearie,' she said. 'I'll take you home.'

'Yes, yes, take me home, Duppy,' whispered Mrs. Mayne. 'Take me away from here . . . '

'I'll get a cab,' said Brett.

'I've got a taxi waiting,' said Mrs. Duppy. 'I guessed she'd come here, you see, when I missed her . . . '

She led her mistress gently over to the iron door. Isobel Mayne made no resistance. She seemed only too glad to go. Without once looking back she allowed Mrs. Duppy to shepherd her through the door, and they heard the tapping stick grow fainter until it faded to silence.

Nutty drew a long breath.

'Lumme,' he muttered, 'the old lady gives yer the creeps, don't she?'

'She *is* a bit weird,' agreed Brett.

'Of course she's crazy, poor old thing,' said Hays.

'Aye' — Macdonald stroked his chin thoughtfully — 'but there's no denying that she hasna been right . . . '

'Did you notice the stick she uses?' asked Hays.

Brett nodded.

'Yes, what about it?' he asked.

'Didn't you see?' Ronnie Hays paused for a moment and then went on deliberately: 'It was a sword-stick . . . '

\* \* \*

Detective-Inspector Hinton was a thin, wiry, dapper man. From the top of his very smooth head to his neat, shining toe-caps he radiated polished efficiency. He looked as if he had just stepped out of a barber's chair, so clean was his chin and so fresh his rather florid cheeks.

He sat in the chair in Angus Macdonald's office, which was usually reserved for important clients, and fingered his stubble of moustache that looked like a caterpillar that had strayed across his upper lip. He had just arrived after an extensive examination of the Regency Theatre which, incidentally, had resulted in precisely nothing. Neither had a previous visit to Isobel Mayne. He was hoping for better results from an interview with the people he had now come to see.

Macdonald, at the telephone, paused in the midst of his conversation and looked over at the Inspector.

'The builders are sending a representative along to the Regency Theatre in the morning to see what wants doing — will that be all right?'

'Oh, yes, sir,' said the Inspector. 'We've finished with the place. There was nothing there to help us, unfortunately.'

'You found nothing?' asked Brett.

'Not a fingerprint or a footmark. The murderer smeared 'em all out.'

'It's an extraordinary business,' said Brett.

'You're right. Somebody seems to have been using the building quite a lot recently.'

'What do ye mean, Inspector?'

Macdonald put the receiver back on its rack and turned round to face the other.

'Well, sir,' said Hinton, 'there are signs that suggest some person has been in and out on several occasions while the place has been shut up . . . '

'What on earth for?' asked Hays.

'We've no idea at present.'

'How could they get in?' demanded Macdonald. 'The keys were at Alexander Mayne's bank until this morning.'

'We verified that,' said Hinton. 'We thought there might be a duplicate set; but the dead man's mother says no.'

'Ye've seen Mrs. Mayne?' asked Macdonald.

'Yes' — Inspector Hinton shrugged his shoulders — 'but we couldn't get much out of her, poor thing. She's very upset about her son's death and also a bit queer in the head — I expect you know that?'

'Aye.'

'Seems to think that her son was killed by some kind of malignant influence that inhabits the old theatre.' Hinton made a slight grimace. 'She says she warned him against re-opening it . . . '

'She did — she warned us all,' said Brett.

'Her husband was murdered in the Regency thirty years ago,' said Macdonald.

'Yes, I've got all that. It can't have any bearing on the present issue.'

'Do you think that some crook has been using the theatre as a hiding-place?' suggested Brett. 'If Mayne had surprised him that might be a motive, mightn't it?'

'Well, it's a possibility,' admitted the Inspector. 'There's one or two chaps I know of on 'the run' who wouldn't stick at murder if they were cornered. An old place like that 'ud be just the kind they'd choose for a 'hide-out'. Been closed for thirty years an' they wouldn't know there was any chance of it being opened.'

'I think you've probably hit it, Clifford,' said Hays.

'I can't think of any other motive,' said Brett.

'There doesn't seem to be one,' grunted Hinton. 'It 'ud explain how they got in an' out, too. An experienced crook with a skeleton-key could do the trick as easy as kiss your hand. By the way, speaking of doors, one of the dressing rooms is barred up and sealed — do you know anything about that?'

'Aye, that was Castleton Mayne's dressing room.'

'Mrs. Mayne sealed it up herself when the theatre was closed. There's a clause in our agreement requiring us to keep the seals intact,' explained Brett.

'Oh, I see.' Hinton nodded. 'I was wondering about that door. Not that it can have anything to do with this business, of course . . . You can see it hasn't been opened for years . . . Well, I don't think I need trouble you gentlemen any more for the present. You'll be hearing from the Coroner's Officer about the inquest . . . '

He picked up his hat, rose to his feet, and crossed to the door.

'Good day, Inspector,' said Macdonald. 'Ye'll let us know if ye discover anything more?'

'You'll hear about it,' said Hinton. 'Good afternoon.'

When he had gone, Macdonald looked at the others.

'Quite a pleasant fellow,' he remarked. 'Ye didna tell him aboot the message on the door . . . '

'There was no need,' said Brett. 'It can't have anything to do with Mayne's murder. I believe Isobel Mayne was behind that message. She was the only person who knew that we'd got the theatre . . . '

'She couldna have done it hersel',' objected Macdonald.

'Perhaps not — though I don't think she's as feeble as she looks. But she may have got someone to do it for her. That woman, Duppy, for instance.'

The door opened and Nutty Potts came in. His face was aglow with excitement.

''Ere — 'ave yer seen the evenin' papers?' he cried, waving one under their noses. 'Look . . . right across the front page . . . see?'

'Mayne's murder?' asked Brett.

'Yes,' said the little man, 'with a 'istory o' the Regency Theatre, an' 'alf a column about the show. Cor blimey! talk about publicity — yer couldn't wish fer no better!'

He spread the newspaper out on the desk.

'I thought there'd be a lot about it,' remarked Macdonald. 'The theatre was swarming with reporters before we left.'

'There ain't nothing like a real juicy murder ter get the public interested,' said Nutty, with satisfaction, 'an' when yer add a 'aunted theatre as well — lumme, it's a cinch! I reckon this is goin' ter be worth quids an' quids to us.'

'They've even picked out an old photograph of Castleton Mayne,' said Brett, pointing to the front page. 'Alexander wasn't very like his father, was he?'

'The features are the same,' said Macdonald, 'but he was no so good-looking . . .'

'I wonder who killed him?' murmured Ronnie Hays, thoughtfully.

Before anyone could answer him there was a tap on the door and Olivia Winter came in.

'Excuse me, Mr. Brett,' she said. 'There's a man in the outer office who wants to see you. He says it's urgent.'

'Who is he?' asked Brett.

'He didn't give any name — he said it

was about the murder at the Regency Theatre . . .'

'Oh, heck!' Brett sighed wearily. 'I'll bet it's another reporter. I can't see any more . . .'

'I don't think he's a reporter,' said the secretary. She stopped abruptly, her eyes fixed on the newspaper spread out on the desk. 'Oh!' she whispered, and her face turned white.

'What's the matter?' asked Brett.

She took a step forward and pointed to the photograph of Castleton Mayne.

'That's the man,' she said.

They stared at her.

'That's impossible,' said Brett

'But it *is*, Mr. Brett,' she persisted. 'I'm sure it is. He's in the outer office now . . .'

'Blimey!'

'I'll go and see,' said Brett.

He went over to the door and disappeared. Presently, after a few seconds, he called: 'There's nobody here, Miss Winter — nobody at all.'

'He *was* there,' she answered. 'He *was* there, Mr. Brett — the man in the photograph . . . '

'That's the photograph of Castleton Mayne, Miss Winter,' said Macdonald, impatiently. 'And he was murdered thirty years ago.'

'I don't care,' she said, and there was horror in her voice, 'he was there — he spoke to me. It was the same man . . . '

'Yer must've been seein' thin's,' said Nutty.

'I tell you he was there,' she cried, hysterically. 'Oh, why did you re-open the Regency? There was something — horrible — locked up in that old building and now — you've let it out . . . '

'Miss Winter, you're talking nonsense,' said Macdonald, roughly.

'I'm not . . . I'm not!'

'Macdonald!' Brett's voice called urgently, and they heard his footsteps crossing the outer office hurriedly. The next moment he was back in the office holding something in his hand.

'Macdonald, look at this. Look at it . . . it was on Miss Winter's desk . . . '

Olivia screamed. It was not a loud scream, but a hoarse, strangled cry of fear. Macdonald stared at the thing in Brett's hand.

'It's . . . it's a knife,' he whispered, incredulously. 'A knife with blood on it . . . '

'Yes,' said Brett, grimly. 'I think it's the knife that killed Alexander Mayne . . . '

# 7

Phillip Defoe sat at ease in a comfortable chair. A bottle of John Haig, a siphon of soda, and a glass, stood on a silver tray on a small table by his side, and the radio was playing softly. He stared thoughtfully at the electric fire, chewing at the cigar between his teeth. Suddenly, in the stillness of the flat, a bell rang softly. Defoe, glancing at the clock, rose to his feet, and walked out into the hall. When he opened the front door Madeleine Peters came in quickly.

'Phillip,' she said a little breathlessly, 'have you seen the evening papers?'

'Yes,' he nodded.

'Alexander Mayne was murdered — this morning — in the Regency Theatre . . . ' she said, excitedly. Again he nodded.

'I know, my dear, I know,' he answered. 'Come into the sitting room . . . '

'What do you mean — you *know*?' she

demanded as she followed him, and there was fear in her voice.

'I've seen the papers,' he said, casually.

'Oh!' There was relief in her voice, and Defoe smiled.

'What did you think I meant, Madeleine?' he asked. He took her by the shoulders and looked into her face. 'You surely didn't imagine that I had anything to do with this murder,' he said softly, 'or did you?'

'No — no, of course not,' she answered, but her eyes refused to meet his. He let go her shoulders and turned away.

'You seem to be a little nervy, my dear,' he said, with the hint of a sneer. 'Sit down and have a drink.'

She slipped off her fur coat and threw it over the back of the settee.

'I will — a large whisky,' she answered. 'Make it neat.'

He poured out a generous portion of Haig, and brought the drink over to her.

She swallowed half of it at a gulp.

'It gave me a shock to see all this in the papers,' she said, 'after what we'd been talking about . . . '

'You thought I was at the bottom of it?' he asked, carefully pouring himself a drink.

'No — no, but I . . . '

'Come, come,' he said, 'you might as well admit it. You have a very expressive face, Madeleine — except when you are on the stage.'

She finished the remainder of her whisky and held out the glass for more.

'*Did* you have anything to do with it?' she asked.

'Would I be so foolish as to tell you if I had?' he replied, taking the glass from her. 'You would go rushing off to the police . . . '

'I wouldn't,' she denied, quickly.

'Oh, you would probably be sorry for it afterwards, but that would be too late. However, you can set your mind at rest. I did *not* kill this man Mayne.'

'Who could have done it?' she said, frowning.

He shrugged his shoulders and began to refill her glass.

'I've no more idea than you have,' he

said. 'Unless, of course, it was you.'

'*Me!*' She stared at him in consternation. 'Don't be ridiculous. Why should I . . . ?'

'You were ready enough to suspect me,' he answered. 'You can hardly be surprised if I return the compliment.'

'You're crazy,' she exclaimed. 'Of course I had nothing to do with it . . . '

'Yes,' he murmured, 'I think, perhaps, you lack the courage to kill.'

'Why do you suppose Mayne *was* killed?' she asked.

He held out the glass of whisky and she took it. This time she did not drink at once, but sat twisting the glass about in her fingers.

'It's queer, you know, Phillip,' she said. 'He'd only just opened the theatre — and somebody kills him . . . '

He nodded and sipped his whisky.

'Yes,' he agreed, 'yes, very queer, as you say. I wonder . . . ?' He stopped.

'What do you wonder?' she asked, sharply.

'I wonder if the person who rang you up and told you that Brett had got the

Regency — the voice that you could not identify — had anything to do with the murder?'

'I can't see why . . . ' she began.

'It is strange that someone should have rung you up and told you,' went on Defoe, with a puzzled frown. 'It has worried me. I do not understand how they could have known so quickly.'

'I don't suppose Brett kept it a secret,' she said.

'No — not from his friends, but . . . '

'It can't have been one of them. None of them would have told me. They disliked me.'

'Yes — they dislike you, and they know that you dislike Brett. If, for some reason of their own, they wished to try and stop this deal going through . . . '

'The deal *had* gone through,' she protested, but he shook his head.

'No, no — it hadn't. If you remember, the voice told you that the agreement was being signed in the morning. If they rang up in the hope that you or I would, in some way, stop the signing . . . '

'Why should anyone think we'd want to?' she asked.

'I don't know . . . '

'And how did they expect we *could* stop Brett getting the theatre?'

'They may have thought we'd do something — and then when we didn't, they took matters into their own hands and killed Mayne.'

'But that wouldn't stop Brett getting the Regency. The agreement was signed before Mayne was killed.'

'Yes, luckily for Brett. But supposing this person didn't know that?'

'Who would go to the length of killing Mayne just to stop Clifford Brett getting the Regency Theatre?'

'My dear,' he said, 'a few minutes ago you thought *I* had.'

'That's different,' she retorted, 'you've got a reason . . . '

'This unknown person who whispers on telephones may have a reason too — perhaps a stronger reason than mine.'

'What?'

'It might be a purely private reason . . . '

112

'An enemy of Mayne's you mean?'

'Or of Brett's,' said Defoe.

She thought for a moment and then she shrugged her shoulders.

'Well, it's given them a lot of publicity,' she said.

'And the show,' he remarked, 'it will be very useful when I take it over.'

'If you ever get the chance,' she said, doubtfully.

He drained his whisky.

'I shall make the chance,' he answered.

* * *

There was a conference that evening at Clifford Brett's flat. Keith, Ronnie Hays, Nutty Potts, Macdonald, and Tangye Ward wedged themselves into the tiny sitting room, occupying such chairs as were available.

'You'll have whisky, of course, Mac?' said Brett, pouring out drinks at a side table.

'Aye, an' I'll have it as whisky was meant to be drunk — neat!' answered Macdonald.

Brett poured out three fingers of John Haig.

'Beer for you, Nutty?'

'Please, Mr. Brett.'

'Can I have some more orange in this gin, please?' asked Tangye.

'Of course — give her some more, Keith, will you?'

Keith took the glass from the girl's hand and went over to the drinks table.

'What a day!' remarked Ronnie Hays, draping his long legs over the arm of a chair. 'A murder *and* a ghost — phew!'

'You'll never get me to believe that it was a ghost that put that knife on Miss Winter's desk,' said Brett.

'She's quite convinced that it was the ghost of Castleton Mayne,' said Keith. He carried the gin and orange back to Tangye.

'Aye — an' in spite of the fright she got there was a glint of triumph in her eye because her warnings had been justified,' said Macdonald.

'She couldn't possibly have known,' said Tangye.

'Do you think Mrs. Mayne's prophecy

was a coincidence, too?' said Macdonald.

'I'm not so sure about *that*,' said Brett.

'You don't think she could have had anything to do with it, surely?' said Tangye.

'I don't know,' said Brett, thoughtfully.

'The whole thing is — why should anyone want to kill Alexander Mayne?' said Keith.

'What does Inspector Hinton think?' asked Tangye.

'That's rather difficult to tell,' answered Brett. 'He doesn't say very much.'

'I don't think he knows what to say,' said Hays.

'Cor lumme! I don't wonder, neither,' put in Nutty.

'He hasna had much time, ye know,' said Macdonald. 'It only happened this morning.'

'That's true.' Keith drank some whisky and looked up. 'You were at the theatre before any of us, Nutty. Did you see anybody hanging about?'

The little man shook his head.

'Not a blinkin' soul,' he declared. ''Inton asked me that.'

'It must have been a near thing that you didn't run into the murderer, Nutty,' said Brett. 'Mayne could only have been killed a few minutes before you arrived.'

'Blimey, don't I know it?' said Nutty, with feeling. 'Every time I think of it I go goosey all over.'

'I think I shall always feel 'goosey' whenever I go into the Regency,' said Tangye, with a little shudder.

'Not when it's all cleaned and freshened up, you won't,' said Brett.

'I shall never forget that moment — on the stage — when I thought it was water — until I looked at my hand,' she said.

'Well, look here, let's talk about something else,' said Brett. 'This isn't very profitable. Mayne was murdered and the police have the matter in hand. Let's leave it to them. It's not our business.'

'You can't help being curious,' said Hays.

'I know, but it doesn't get us anywhere . . . '

There was a knock at the front door, and Brett broke off and frowned.

'Who the deuce can that be?' he said.

'All right, I'll go.'

He put down his glass on the mantelpiece and went out into the little hall. Opening the door he saw a tall figure outside.

'Mrs. Mayne!' he exclaimed in surprise.

'May I come in?' she said. 'I wish to speak to you.'

'Yes, of course.' He ushered her into the hall and shut the door. 'This way.'

He took her into the sitting room.

'I think you know everybody except Miss Ward,' he said. 'Tangye, this is Mrs. Isobel Mayne.'

'How do you do?' said Tangye.

'Sit down, Mrs. Mayne,' said Brett.

The gaunt woman shook her head.

'I shall not be staying, Mr. Brett,' she answered. 'I have come to make an appeal to you. Please give up this idea of re-opening the Regency Theatre. There is still time.'

'I can't,' he replied. 'I'm sorry . . . '

'You have seen the result already,' she continued swiftly and urgently. 'Surely you do not want to put other lives in jeopardy?'

'But — Mrs. Mayne, that is ridiculous . . . '

'My son's death was not — ridiculous,' she retorted.

'If you can give us any really sensible reason why we shouldn't re-open . . . ' began Brett.

'Sensible reason?' she echoed. 'The reason I have already given you is sensible. Have you not had sufficient proof yet? Must others die to convince you?'

'Why should others die?' asked Keith, quietly.

She made an impatient gesture. 'I have already told you . . . '

'But, Mrs. Mayne,' said Macdonald, 'what you believe isna practical.'

'It was practical enough to kill my son,' she answered.

'Your son was killed by a human agency, Mrs. Mayne,' said Brett, 'not by these malignant forces which you imagine exist . . . '

'Do you know who killed my son?' she asked.

'Well, no . . . '

'Then you cannot say how he died,' she declared.

'But . . . '

'These forces, which you think I imagine,' she went on, taking no notice of the interruption, 'can use a human being to bring about their desires. Marsden was possessed by them when he killed my husband, and they left him — mad . . . Take care they do not do the same by one of you.' Her piercing eyes turned towards Tangye and she fixed the girl with a long, penetrating stare. 'That girl there,' she continued, 'she is young and pretty. Supposing you suddenly saw her with her face distorted and ugly with hate and her eyes shining with evil . . . '

'Oh, don't — please don't!' cried Tangye, suddenly terrified.

'It could happen,' said Mrs. Mayne, 'if you do not heed what I say. Or perhaps *she* will see the lust to kill in one of *your* faces . . . '

The atmosphere in the little room was suddenly charged with terror. Long afterwards Tangye remembered that scene and the old woman's voice, and even then, when there was nothing more to fear, the memory brought back all her terror of that moment. Clifford Brett's matter-of-fact voice broke the spell.

'I'm sure you're quite sincere in your belief, Mrs. Mayne,' he said, 'but it's really absurd . . . '

She looked at him. Behind the deep-set eyes he caught a glimpse of something he could not define. An expression? It was hardly that. Something less tangible . . .

'You refuse, then, Mr. Brett, to give up this project — in spite of my warning and what you have already seen?'

'Yes,' he answered, 'I'm afraid I must.'

She sighed and her tall figure seemed to shrink. Quite calmly she turned away and walked slowly to the door.

'I can do no more,' she said. 'You will be sorry, but by then it will be too late. When death comes again — don't forget that I warned you . . . '

# 8

The two weeks immediately following the murder of Alexander Mayne was a busy time. The old Regency Theatre resounded to the noise of hammering and sawing, the raucous voices of workmen, and all the bustle and confusion that an army of people, all engaged in doing a different job of work, can make. Outside, pipes, belching forth scalding steam, and held by men in swaying cradles, snaked up the front of the building, and under their hissing jets the soot and grime peeled away from the stone and brick, restoring it to something approaching its pristine glory.

A contingent of cleaners dealt with the gold scrollwork on the sweeping front of circle and gallery, walls and ceiling, and under their energetic efforts the ravages of time and damp disappeared and the gold and the old rose of paint and carpets and hangings glowed with colour again.

Gradually the beauty that for thirty years had been hidden under a layer of dirt and dust became visible once more.

During all this time rehearsals for the show were carried on in a room hired for the purpose in Oxford Street, Clifford Brett spending his time dashing back and forth between the rehearsal-room and the Regency Theatre. At last the restoration had advanced sufficiently for the company to rehearse on the stage of the theatre, and here they found that the dimensions of the Oxford Street room had been something of a disadvantage. Half-way through the opening number, Brett stopped them.

'Hold it — hold it, everybody, please,' he called. 'Listen. You've been running through these numbers in a rehearsal-room where there wasn't much space. Now you're on a stage it's different. You've got more room and you'll have to spread out more. And don't forget — you'll have three shallow steps to come down . . . Victor!'

'Yes, Mr. Brett?' Victor Price came down to the floats.

'Aren't those two chairs you've got marking that entrance a bit close together?'

'They're right according to the scenic artist's measurements,' said Price.

'They seem a bit narrow to me,' said Brett, frowning. 'Oh, well, never mind. Come along — let's take that opening number again . . . '

Keith Gilbert began the introduction and then the most appalling row broke out in the flies; a loud hammering that drowned everything.

'Oh, heck!' groaned Brett. 'Must they do that just now?'

Victor Price looked up.

'Hi — you up there!' he shouted, but nobody took any notice. The hammering continued with unabated force. Price filled his lungs with more air and tried again.

'You up there!' he yelled, 'can't you hear me?'

The hammering ceased, and a voice answered faintly: '*Me?*'

'Yes, you,' shouted Price.

'Wotcher want?' demanded the voice.

'Can't you cut out the noise?'

'Got ter get the job done, ain't I?' demanded the voice.

'Can't you get on with something that makes a little less row?' suggested Brett.

The owner of the voice appeared to be considering this, for there was a silence before he said: 'Well, I s'pose I could . . . O.K., guv'nor.'

Brett gave a sigh of relief.

'All right,' he said, 'carry on.'

The number was half-way through when Clifford Brett became aware that someone was standing beside him. He looked round and saw a small, wizened man with a wrinkled face and an almost completely bald head. He was very shabbily dressed and carried an old cloth cap which he twisted nervously in rather dirty and very knobbly hands. Seeing that Brett had noticed him he bent down and said, in a hoarse whisper: 'Could I 'ave a word with yer, sir?'

'Who are you — what do you want?' answered Brett.

'They sent me along from Macdonald's agency, sir,' said the old man. 'Yer Mr.

Brett, ain't yer, sir?'

'Yes.'

'Me name's Savernick, sir,' went on the man. 'You was wantin' a stage doorkeeper . . . '

'You'd better see my stage manager,' said Brett.

'I used ter be a stage 'and 'ere in the time o' Mr. Castleton Mayne, sir — 'im what was murdered . . . '

'The deuce you did!' exclaimed Brett. 'How old are you?'

'Sixty-seven, sir.'

'Wait until this number finishes and I'll get hold of my stage manager,' said Brett.

The queer little man thanked him and stood quietly waiting. When the number came to an end, Brett called Victor Price.

'This man's come from Macdonald's after the job of stage doorkeeper,' he said. 'Have a word with him, will you?'

The stage manager nodded and took the little man away. Brett looked round for Tangye, but the girl was nowhere to be seen. He called her and presently she came running across the stage.

'I'm sorry, Mr. Brett,' she apologized,

breathlessly. 'I didn't think you wanted me yet.'

'I want to do your number with the girls — the bathing suit number,' said Brett. He raised his voice and called: 'All ready there? We'll do the bathing number.'

They went right through it. Brett made no comment until it was over and then he said: 'O.K. That's fine. Very nice, Tangye.'

She flushed with pleasure at the praise.

'Smashin',' remarked a voice at Brett's elbow. He turned to find Nutty beside him.

'Hello,' he said, 'where have you been?'

'Sittin' at the back o' the stalls. Place looks a bit different now, don't it?'

'It'll look better still when it's finished,' said Brett.

'I wonder if they'll ever find out who did in Mayne?' remarked Nutty, thoughtfully.

'I don't know,' answered Brett. 'I've heard nothing from Hinton since I gave him that knife. That was a fortnight ago . . . Look here, Nutty, you go back to the rear of the stalls and let me get on with this rehearsal . . . '

'Okey doke,' agreed Nutty, cheerfully. 'I'm goin' ter find Maysie Sheringham an' see if she'll come out to lunch.'

'I wish you'd leave the girl alone,' growled Brett.

'Wot — when she's just beginnin' ter come round?' demanded Nutty. 'Cor lumme, she don't walk away now when I speaks to 'er — she just shuts 'er eyes an' sighs!'

'Mr. Brett,' Tangye called from the stage, and he looked up.

'Yes?' he said.

'Can I slip out for a minute or two? I want to do some shopping. I won't be long . . . '

He nodded. 'All right. Don't hurry. I shan't want you for a bit now.'

She thanked him and hurried away. Brett called Maysie Sheringham and she began a comedy number with the chorus. They had scarcely started when a scream reached them from somewhere outside in the passage leading to the stage door.

'What was that?' exclaimed Brett, sharply. 'Who screamed?'

He was answered by Keith Gilbert's voice.

'Clifford . . . Clifford, come here quickly.'

Brett ran round and through the pass-door. When he reached the passage he found an excited group of people gathered round someone lying on the floor. It was Tangye.

'She's fainted,' said Keith in reply to his query.

'Why — what happened?' asked Brett.

'I don't know — I'd just come in the stage door. I found her lying here.' Keith's face was worried.

'We'd better do something . . .'

'It's all right, she's coming round,' said Brett. He knelt down beside the girl, who was stirring slightly. 'All right, Tangye,' he said. 'There's nothing to be afraid of. What happened?'

'Oh,' she murmured, faintly. 'It — it frightened me . . .'

'What did? What frightened you?' asked Keith, anxiously.

'The — the knocking . . .'

'What knocking?'

She sat up gingerly and stared across the passage at the door of the sealed dressing room.

'It came from there,' she said, 'from inside — just as I was passing the door . . . '

'That's the sealed room,' said Brett. 'There couldn't be anyone in there . . . '

'I know — that's what frightened me,' she answered. 'That's why it was — it was so *horrible*. There couldn't be, but there was — somebody who was knocking — as though . . . ' She paused, and then went on, almost inaudibly: '*As though they wanted to be let out — !*'

A queer kind of hush filled the dark and narrow passage, and unconsciously everybody looked at the locked and sealed door that had once been Castleton Mayne's dressing room. Clifford Brett, in spite of his scepticism, felt a cold creeping of the flesh. He pulled himself together quickly.

'There couldn't possibly be anyone in there, Tangye,' he said, 'you must have been mistaken . . . '

'I wasn't,' she answered. 'Somebody

knocked on the inside of that door. I was close to it — I heard it plainly . . . '

'There's not a sound inside there now,' remarked Brett, impatiently. 'How could anyone get in there? Look at these seals' — he touched them with his finger — 'they're just as they were when they were put on thirty years ago . . . '

'Perhaps you heard something outside in the street that sounded as if it came from the dressing-room?' suggested Keith.

Tangye shook her head.

'It came from inside that room,' she declared, stubbornly. 'The knocking was repeated several times — like someone banging with their fist on the panel of the door . . . '

Victor Price hurried forward with a chair and Tangye sat down. She was still a little shaky and her face was pale. She smiled her thanks.

'I know what it was,' said Ronnie Hays, suddenly.

'What?' asked Brett.

'One of the workmen in another part of the building, of course,' he answered. 'Sound travels along pipes and things . . . '

Brett's face cleared.

'That's it,' he said. 'That's what it must have been . . . '

'That was the old guvnor's room, that was,' remarked a voice, and Brett, looking round, saw Savernick peering through the crowd.

'Yes, we know that,' said Brett. 'How are you feeling now, Tangye?'

'I'm — I'm all right,' she said, but she didn't look it.

'I'll slip along to the pub at the corner and get you a spot of brandy,' said Keith.

'Oh, no — please don't bother . . . ' she began, but he was already on his way.

'The old guv'nor used ter send me to that pub,' said Savernick. 'Whisky 'e used ter drink. I remember the night 'e was murdered . . . '

'That'll do,' said Brett, sharply. He turned to face the others. 'Will you all go back to the stage, please,' he continued, 'and we'll get on with the rehearsal.'

They moved away, whispering among themselves, and in a few seconds the passage was empty except for Brett,

Tangye, and Hays.

'You'd better stop where you are for a bit, Tangye,' said Hays. 'I'll stay with you.'

'That's right, Ronnie,' agreed Brett. 'Look after her. I must get on with this rehearsal . . .'

He hurried away round the bend in the passage.

'He thinks I imagined it,' said Tangye, 'but I didn't. I really did hear somebody knocking inside that room.'

'But how could you?' he protested. 'The door hasn't been opened since the theatre was closed down.'

'I know it sounds impossible,' she persisted, 'but it happened.'

'Well, a lot of queer things *have* happened, I'll admit,' he said, 'but . . .' He shook his head instead of finishing the sentence.

'There's something very queer going on here,' said Tangye, seriously, 'and I believe it's all part of the same thing. That message on your door, and the man who came to Mr. Macdonald's office and left that knife, and Alexander Mayne's murder . . .'

Keith Gilbert's voice broke into the middle of her sentence.

'Here you are, Tangye.' He came hurrying up to them carrying a glass of amber liquid. 'Drink this. It'll put you right in no time.'

She took the glass from him with a smile.

'You shouldn't have gone to all that trouble,' she said.

'No trouble,' declared Keith. His eyes twinkled. 'I had one myself . . . '

The sound of the piano came to their ears from the stage.

'They've started rehearsing again,' said Tangye. She half rose from her chair. 'I ought to go back in case I'm wanted . . . '

'You stay where you are,' said Gilbert, gently pushing her back. 'Finish that brandy — every drop of it.'

He looked round as he heard somebody approaching. It was Olivia Winter.

'Good morning,' she greeted, brightly. 'Is Mr. Brett . . . ?' She stopped as she caught sight of the glass in the girl's hand.

'What's happened?' she asked, sharply.

'Miss Ward's had rather a nasty shock,' said Keith.

'Oh?' The secretary looked quickly from one to the other. 'What sort of a shock?'

Keith told her. The expression of her face changed as she listened. It became grave and slightly alarmed.

'Of course,' Keith ended, 'Miss Ward must have been mistaken.'

'Do you think so?' said Olivia.

'Obviously. Nothing human could have got in there, Miss Winter. You don't believe it was a ghost, do you?'

'What was it that came to the office that afternoon — the afternoon following the murder? And left that knife . . . '

'It wasn't Castleton Mayne's ghost, if that's what you're suggesting,' said Ronnie Hays.

'Wasn't it?' Olivia Winter looked at him steadily. 'There was nobody there when Mr. Brett went into the outer office to look — and the lift man, who was on duty all the time, swears that nobody came or went out.'

'But, Miss Winter . . . '

'And yet he *was* there — in my office — I saw him as plainly as I can see you now. And he was the man whose photograph was in the paper — Castleton Mayne!'

'There must be some explanation,' said Hays.

'There is,' retorted Olivia, 'but none of you will accept it.' She turned away. 'I must go and find Mr. Brett. Miss Ward — I should keep as far away as possible from that sealed dressing room in future, if I were you,' she said, and hurried away.

'She really believes that it was the ghost of Castleton Mayne, you know,' said Keith, looking after her.

'Oh, don't let's talk about it anymore,' said Tangye. 'Let's go back to the stage. It's getting very cold out here . . . '

When they reached the stage Maysie Sheringham and the chorus were in the middle of a number. They watched from the side until it was over and then they were joined by Brett.

'How are you feeling now, Tangye?' he inquired.

'Fine,' she answered.

'Then we may as well run through the . . . Yes, what is it, Victor?'

'It's about that man, Savernick, Mr. Brett,' said the stage manager. 'He seems all right. I've told him to start tomorrow morning.'

'Oh, good,' said Brett. 'Will you tell Mr. Macdonald, Miss Winter?' he added to the secretary, who was standing beside him.

'Tell Mr. Macdonald what, Mr. Brett?' she asked.

'We've engaged that man you sent along for stage doorkeeper . . . '

She looked at him with a puzzled expression.

'What man?' she asked.

'Savernick,' he replied. 'You sent him here from the office . . . '

'There must be some mistake, Mr. Brett,' she said. 'We never sent anybody . . . '

# 9

Phillip Defoe sat at his desk in the office next door to the Rialto Theatre. He was chewing on the end of a cigar which had gone out, and there was a worried expression on his face. The telephone bell rang and he reached out an arm to the receiver.

'Hello,' he said, softly. 'Defoe speaking . . . Oh, it's you. Well, what happened?'

The telephone chattered rapidly.

'I thought you'd fix it,' said Defoe. 'You'd better not come here. I'll meet you at the main bookstall at Waterloo at — let me see — five-thirty. Yes, yes, I'll bring it with me.'

He hung the receiver back on its rack and leaned back in his chair. There was a little smile on his thick lips and he looked as though something had pleased him.

Madeleine Peters, reclining gracefully in a big leather chair facing the desk, raised her eyebrows slightly.

'I gather from that little conversation,' she remarked, 'that it worked?'

'Yes,' he nodded. 'Now we are all set for the — finale.'

'Can't be too soon for me,' she said.

'What an impatient girl you are, Madeleine,' he murmured.

'I'm sick of all this about the Regency Theatre and Tangye Ward,' she declared. 'You can't pick up a newspaper without seeing a lot of rubbish about one or the other . . . '

'Their publicity has certainly been marvellous,' he said.

'Tangye Ward!' she burst out. 'A tuppenny-ha'penny little chorus girl . . . That's all she is.'

'That's all she *was*,' he corrected.

'Tangye — Tangye . . . Did you ever hear such a silly name?' She snapped her fingers. 'It sounds like an orange!'

'From a really unprejudiced point of view, my dear,' he said, 'I think it's rather an attractive name.'

'I suppose you think she's an attractive girl?' she snapped.

'Very.'

'Huh!'

'Evidently you disagree,' he said. His eyes were amused. 'I suppose all attraction is a matter of opinion. The public will, I think, agree with me . . . '

'If it ever has the chance of seeing her,' said Madeleine.

'Which, of course, it won't,' he answered.

'Do you think this plan of yours will succeed?' she asked.

'Of course. It is so simple it can't fail.'

'You're not afraid that somebody might suspect that it was you?'

'If there was the slightest chance of that,' he answered, 'I assure you that I should have nothing more to do with it. My reputation . . . '

'Don't make me laugh,' she interrupted.

'I fail to see anything humorous in that . . . ' he began.

'You've got the worst reputation in the theatre business,' she retorted, 'and you know it.'

'People are jealous of my success.'

'No, Phillip,' she said, quickly. 'They

just dislike the methods by which you attain it.'

He was annoyed. His face darkened and his eyes narrowed.

'There is a saying, I think,' he said easily, 'something about a pot and a kettle — isn't that so?'

'Meaning?' she demanded.

'You are not — altogether — scrupulous yourself.'

'I never pretended to be,' she said. 'I believe in getting what you want without worrying too much how you get it. But I don't delude myself that I'm any better than I am.'

'You think I do?'

'Well, don't you? What you said just now about your reputation rather proves it.'

'I have a very clear conception of myself, Madeleine,' he said. 'Very clear indeed.'

She rose to her feet languidly, came over to the desk, and took a cigarette from the silver box.

'I'm sure you have, darling,' she agreed as she waited for him to give her a light.

'Unfortunately it's quite a different one to other people's. I know you rather well, you see . . . '

He held out the lighter and she dipped the end of her cigarette in the tiny flame for a second.

'I wonder if you do?' he murmured.

'Yes — very well, Phillip,' she said. 'So well that there are times when I'm a little afraid of you . . . '

He raised his eyebrows. 'My dear — why?'

'Because you're quite ruthless,' she said with a little shrug. 'You'd even sacrifice me to get something you really wanted, and if you couldn't get it any other way, wouldn't you?'

He looked up at her for a few seconds in silence and his face was quite expressionless. Then he reached out and helped himself to a fresh cigar.

'I shouldn't let it worry you,' he said, lightly. 'Let us hope, for your sake, that such a situation will never arise . . . '

★ ★ ★

The rehearsals for the show went forward smoothly. Gradually it was beginning to take shape. Clifford Brett was pleased with it except for one portion in the second half which seemed to drag a little. He discussed it with Ronnie Hays after the company had broken for the day.

'We want something with a punch,' he said, 'after Maysie's number.'

'Something that will get plenty of laughs?' suggested Hays.

'That's the idea,' agreed Brett.

'I'll work something out,' said Ronnie. 'I've done a new duet for Tangye and Clavering — Keith was setting it last night.'

'What happened to Keith after rehearsal this morning?' asked Brett. 'I never saw him go.'

Ronnie grinned.

'He went off somewhere with Tangye,' he said.

'H'm,' remarked Brett. 'Oh, well, she's a very attractive girl.'

'And a very nice one too,' said Hays.

'She's good in the show — Madeleine Peters did us a good turn when she walked out that day.'

'I'll bet she's furious!' Ronnie chuckled.

'And Defoe too, I expect,' said Brett.

'They'll be more furious if the show's a big success . . . '

'*When*, Ronnie. It's going to be . . . Hello, Victor — I thought you'd gone . . . '

'Just going, Mr. Brett,' said Price.

'There's something I wanted to ask you . . . '

'Go ahead.'

'Well, we're going to be awfully short of dressing rooms. Can't we use the one that's locked?'

'Nothing doing, Victor, I'm afraid,' answered Brett, shaking his head. 'That was one of the conditions we had to agree to, to get the theatre. There's a clause in the agreement that it mustn't be opened.'

'Queer idea, isn't it?' said Price.

'Yes, I suppose it is, in a way,' agreed Brett, 'but I can understand how Mrs. Mayne felt about it. I believe everything in there is just as her husband left it when he went down on the stage to make his last entrance.'

'I see . . . Yes, I suppose it's under-standable,' said Price.

'By the way,' said Brett, 'that chap Savernick wasn't sent by Macdonald's at all . . . '

'He wasn't?'

'No, they've never heard of him. You might ask him to-morrow why he said they'd sent him.'

'I will.' Victor Price hesitated. 'I suppose,' he said, after a short pause, 'there's no further news about the murder?'

'We haven't heard anything,' answered Brett.

'Mysterious business, wasn't it?'

'Very . . . '

'We'll hear one day that the police have made an arrest and then we shall know all about it,' said Hays.

'If they ever catch the person who did it,' remarked Price.

'They're pretty good, you know,' said Brett. 'Very few murderers get away with it . . . '

'Perhaps this one's a little bit cleverer than the others,' suggested Price.

'I remember reading once that all murderers think they're so clever that they'll never be caught,' said Hays.

'That's fairly obvious,' remarked Brett. 'If they thought they were going to be found out they wouldn't do it, would they?' He yawned. 'Suppose we make a move? Which way are you going, Ronnie?'

'I'm going to have a bite to eat somewhere and then I'm going home.'

'Come and have a drink first,' said Brett. 'Coming to have one, Victor?'

'Thanks, Mr. Brett — I'll follow you up,' said the stage manager. 'Just got to put the lights out . . .'

He went over to the big switchboard at the side of the stage, and they passed through the iron door and down the steps to the passage leading to the stage door. A few minutes later, Price joined them. He shut the stage door behind him when they were outside, and locked it.

Inside the darkened theatre there was silence for a moment, and then the sound of footsteps crossing the stage broke it. They were soft footsteps, but deliberate and purposeful. They stopped suddenly and somebody laughed; a soft, throaty chuckle that in the stillness and the darkness sounded indescribably — *evil* . . .

★　★　★

Instead of going home after rehearsal was over that day, Tangye Ward had accepted Maysie Sheringham's suggestion that she should accompany Maysie to her flat and have tea. She went with a purpose in view. For the greater part of the afternoon, Tangye had been worrying over a matter of clothes. When they had finished tea she mentioned her problem to Maysie.

'An evening gown?' said Maysie. 'Well, I could lend you one. We're about the same height and build. Come into the bedroom and let's see what there is.'

She led the way into the bedroom and opened her wardrobe. From a hanger she took a flimsy dress and held it out for Tangye's inspection.

'How would this do?' she asked.

'Oh, it's lovely!' said Tangye.

'It's a Lemoine model — I only bought it last week,' said Maysie. 'It ought to suit your colouring. Slip it on . . . '

'May I?'

'Of course. Here you are . . . '

Tangye took off her suit and pulled the dress gently over her head. It fitted her slim figure as though it had been made for her. She looked at herself in the long mirror.

'It's beautiful,' she said.

'You can borrow it, if you like,' said Maysie.

'Can I? It's awfully sweet of you, Maysie.' Tangye turned round in front of the glass and examined her reflection over one shoulder. 'I've only one decent evening gown and I've worn it each time I've been out with Mr. Gilbert.'

'Why don't you call him Keith?' demanded Maysie. ''Mr. Gilbert' sounds so 'Jane Eyreish'.'

'Well, Keith then . . . '

'That's better. How many times have you been out with him?'

'Only twice.'

'H'm . . . third time lucky. That dress ought to do the trick.'

'I don't know what you mean,' said

Tangye, innocently.

'Bring your young man up to scratch,' retorted Maysie, calmly. 'If he can resist you in that dress there's no hope for him. Look, try these shoes on. You'd better have the whole outfit.'

She held out a pair of very high-heeled slippers the colour of the dress.

'It's awfully kind of you, Maysie . . . '

'Nonsense,' said Maysie. 'Where are you going tonight?'

'The Milan.'

'The Milan!' She raised her eyebrows. 'He does you well, I will say that.'

'I rather wish he wouldn't,' said Tangye, bending down and slipping on the shoes. 'I'd just as soon go to some little place that didn't cost so much.'

'Are those shoes comfy?'

'Yes, they fit perfectly . . . You see — I don't know that he can afford it.'

'I don't think any of them are very well off. They're depending on the success of the show.' Maysie took a cigarette from a packet on the dressing table and lit it. 'I feel happier about that now that Madeleine Peters is out of the cast. She was terrible.'

'It's funny how things happen, isn't it?' said Tangye. 'If Madeleine Peters hadn't walked out that day I might still be in the chorus — I might have been in the chorus for years and years . . . '

'And Alexander Mayne might still be alive,' remarked Maysie, seriously, 'because the Regency wouldn't have been re-opened.'

'I wish sometimes that it never had been,' said Tangye. 'I've an odd feeling about it — it *frightens* me.'

'That's because of the murder.'

Tangye shook her head.

'No, it isn't — not entirely,' she said. 'There's something else. You know, Maysie, that knocking I heard *did* come from inside that room.'

'The fact that it's quite impossible makes no difference, I suppose?' said Maysie.

'I couldn't have imagined it . . . '

'Well, *how* do you explain it?'

'I can't.'

'There you are then . . . Look, darling, let me do your hair for you. You're making a frightful mess of it.'

'Will you? I was going to get it done after rehearsal, but they couldn't take me.'

'Give me that comb . . . Now, keep still.' Maysie set to work with capable fingers. 'You've met Mrs. Mayne, haven't you? What's she like?'

'She's terrifying,' answered Tangye. 'She's tall and very thin, with white hair and the queerest eyes. I can't describe them, but when she looks at you it's really frightening.'

'I was talking to a man yesterday who was with Castleton Mayne at the Regency. He said Isobel Mayne was very beautiful.'

'I can quite believe that,' said Tangye. 'You can still see traces of it. She believes the theatre's haunted . . . '

'She's a little queer in the head, isn't she?' said Maysie. She laughed. 'The only ghost I'm interested in is the one that walks on Friday . . . There — now you look really nice.'

She stood back to survey her work. Tangye eyed her reflection critically.

'It looks lovely,' she said. 'Thank you, Maysie.'

'I hope all my efforts are not going to be in vain,' said Maysie. 'What time are you meeting Keith?'

'Half-past seven,' replied Tangye. She glanced at her watch. 'Oh, I shall have to fly . . .'

'Wait a minute,' said Maysie, 'you want an evening bag. You can't use that. Here you are.'

She opened a drawer, took out an evening bag and held it out.

'Maysie, you're a brick,' said Tangye.

'I'll phone for a taxi,' said Maysie. 'Relax — you'll be in plenty of time — anyway, the anxiety of wondering whether you're going to turn up will make him all the keener.'

★ ★ ★

'Cheerio, Ronnie, I'm off,' said Keith, thrusting his head in at the door of the sitting room. 'Are you staying in this evening?'

'No,' said Ronnie Hays, looking up from his work, 'I'm going over to Clifford's later.'

151

'You'll probably be late, then,' said Keith. 'Oh, well — see you when I get back.'

'O.K. Have a good time.'

'You bet,' called Keith from the hall, and a second later the front door slammed. Ronnie Hays went on working. The lyric he was writing was coming along quite well. He crossed out a line that didn't scan and substituted another. That was better. He laid down his pencil and stretched himself, and at that moment the front doorbell rang.

He rose to his feet, went out into the hall, and opened the door. Nutty Potts was standing outside.

'Ello, can I come in, Mr. 'Ays?' he said.

'Of course. Go into the sitting room,' said Ronnie. He shut the door and followed the little man. 'There's some beer over there — help yourself.'

'Thanks.' Nutty went over to the sideboard and opened a bottle of beer. 'Wot I really popped in ter see yer about was Defoe . . . '

'Defoe?'

'Yes.' Nutty nodded and poured out a

glass of beer. 'You goin' ter 'ave one?'

Hays shook his head.

'What's all this about Defoe?' he said.

Nutty took a long drink.

'I got an idea 'es up ter somethin'.'

'Why?'

'Well, I'll tell yer.' Nutty sat on the arm of an easy-chair and looked over the rim of the glass. 'I've got an old aunt what lives just round by the Elephant an' Castle, see? I ain't seen 'er for quite a bit an' I thought I'd pop along arter rehearsing was over an' say 'ow d'yer do ter the old gal. When I left 'er I was just goin' inter the Tube station when who should I see cumin' out but Defoe . . . '

'What was he doing there?' asked Hays.

'Ah!' Nutty looked into his glass and frowned. 'That's what I thought. 'E didn't see me, an' I thought I'd foller 'im an' find out where 'e went. Yer see, the old Elephant ain't the sort o' place yer'd expect ter find a posh bloke like Defoe wanderin' about . . . '

'Go on, what happened? Where did he go?'

'I'm tellin' yer, ain't I? I follered 'im to

a little shop in a side street close to where me aunt lives . . . '

'What kind of a shop?' asked Hays.

'Now we're comin' to it,' answered Nutty. 'It was an ironmonger's — only a small place, yer understand? His nibs wasn't in there very long, an' when 'e come out I waited until 'e'd got well away an' then I popped in myself. The feller what keeps the shop knows me on account o' me aunt, see? An' when 'e told me what Defoe 'ad been after . . . '

He paused and took another draught of beer.

'Well, what *had* he been after?' demanded Ronnie, impatiently.

'A key,' answered Nutty, impressively. ''E 'ad a key cut from the impression of a lock what 'e'd brought in the day before . . . '

'I can't see anything in that,' said Hays. 'Why shouldn't he?'

'Well, I think it's queer,' said Nutty. 'Why should a bloke like Defoe go all the way ter the Elephant ter get a key cut? Eh? If it was on the square wouldn't 'e be more likely ter send round ter the nearest shop to 'is flat or 'is office?'

'H'm — I suppose he would,' agreed Hays.

''Course 'e would,' declared Nutty. 'An' what's more, 'e gave a false name. 'E called 'isself Robinson.'

'Did he, by Jove!' exclaimed Hays. 'That *does* look suspicious. But what could this key be for?'

'I'll tell yer what I think it is,' said Nutty. 'I think it's a key that will open the stage door of the Regency.'

'What would Defoe want that for?'

'I don't know, but there's some funny business goin' on. Somebody's been prowlin' about the place, ain't they? 'Ow do we know that Defoe ain't at the bottom of it?'

Ronnie Hays took a cigarette from the box on the piano, lit it, and began to pace up and down the room.

'I believe you've hit on something,' he said, after a moment. 'We must tell Clifford about this. I'm going round to see him presently. How about coming with me?'

'Okey doke.'

155

'I can't see what reason Defoe could possibly have for wanting to get into the Regency Theatre . . . '

Nutty emptied his glass.

'Yer must admit it's fishy,' he said.

Hays nodded thoughtfully.

'Yes,' he answered, 'I do . . . I think it's very fishy.'

# 10

Tangye leaned back in the taxi and sighed contentedly.

'You know,' she said, looking sideways at Keith Gilbert, 'I can't help thinking sometimes that this is all a dream. One day I'll wake up and find that it never really happened . . .'

'If it's a dream we're all in it,' he answered.

'I never thought I would ever be a star in a West End show . . .'

'I never thought I'd ever write the music for one,' he retorted. 'When Clifford, Ronnie and I used to talk about this show during the war, the chance of it ever coming to anything seemed very remote. Even when we were demobbed it still seemed pretty hopeless — until we ran into Nutty one day. He made everything possible, bless him.'

'He's a dear . . .'

'Yes — I'm very fond of old Nutty. We all are.'

The taxi slowed down and drew into the kerb.

'Here we are,' said Keith.

He got out and helped the girl down on to the pavement. When he paid the driver and the taxi started to move off he led the way into the block of flats.

'We're lucky,' he said, 'the lift's down. In you go.'

He followed her into the tiny lift, shut the gate, and pressed the button for the third floor.

'It's been a lovely evening,' murmured Tangye as the lift shot upwards.

'It still is a lovely evening,' he corrected. 'It's quite early yet . . .'

'It's ten o'clock,' she said, glancing at her watch. 'I shan't be able to stay very long . . .'

'Tired?' he asked.

'Well, yes, I am a little,' she confessed.

'Rehearsing all day takes it out of you, doesn't it?' he said. 'Well, just have a drink and say 'hello' to Ronnie and then I'll take you home.'

But when they reached the door of the flat there was no light to be seen. The glass fanlight above the front door was dark.

'H'm, it looks as though Ronnie must be out,' remarked Keith. 'Never mind.' He opened the door with his key. 'Go in,' he said, and pressed down the switch. The light in the hall came on and he opened the door of the sitting room.

'There we are,' he said. 'Just sit down and relax and I'll get you a drink . . . What'll it be? Gin — whisky?'

'A gin and orange, please,' she said, 'with plenty of soda. I'm terribly thirsty.'

'Help yourself to cigarettes — they're in that box beside you,' he said.

'Thank you.' She took a cigarette and he lit it for her. 'You were very lucky to get this flat. How did you manage it?'

'A fellow I knew in the army got a job in Canada and let us have the remainder of his lease,' he answered, busying himself at the sideboard.

She laughed.

'As simple as that?' she said.

'As simple as that,' he agreed. 'Here's

your gin with lots of soda.'

He poured himself out a whisky.

'Here's success to you, Tangye — and to the show.'

'I *do* hope it will be a success,' she said, sincerely.

'It will,' he said, confidently.

'Ronnie's written some good stuff and Clifford knows his job backwards. He's a first-rate producer.'

'The music doesn't enter into it, I suppose?' she said.

'Well, yes — of course . . . Do you like it?'

'I think it's lovely,' she answered, enthusiastically.

He flushed with pleasure.

'Do you — *really?*' he said, eagerly. 'I've just done a new number — a duet for you and Clavering in the second half — '

He went quickly over to the piano.

'Have you got it there?' she asked. 'Do let me hear it.'

'We'll try it over together, shall we?' he said, rummaging among the litter on the piano top.

'All right.' She got up and joined him.

'Here it is,' he said.

'Put your glass down on the piano top. I'm afraid this is a bit of a scrawl.' He opened the music and set it up on the rack. 'Can you read it?'

'Yes, I think so,' she said, leaning over his shoulder.

He began to play. She hummed the melody at first and then they sang it through together.

'Do you like it?' asked Keith.

'Yes, very much,' she said.

He went on playing softly, drifting from one number out of the show to another. She went back to her chair and sat watching him. He began to play the theme song.

'I love that number you're playing,' she said.

'Do you?' He continued to play. 'I rather like it myself . . . '

There was a pause. Then he said in a low voice that was barely audible above the piano: 'Tangye — '

'Yes?'

'Do you remember the day when Clifford came back with the news that

161

we'd got the Regency?'

'Yes — I don't think I'll ever forget that day. The most wonderful thing that ever happened to me happened that day . . . '

'Something happened to me, too.'

'To you?'

'Yes . . . '

Again there was silence except for the soft sound of the piano.

'What . . . happened to you?' she asked.

He didn't answer immediately.

'Do you know that sonnet of Shakespeare's which begins: 'So are you to my thoughts as food to life, or as sweet-seasoned showers are to the ground'?' he said at last.

'Yes . . . why — why did you ask me that?'

'Because . . . that's . . . that's how I feel . . . about you . . . ' His hands were still moving gently over the keys. The melody he was playing was soft and sweet. 'I . . . I can't find words of my own, you see . . . I have to borrow Shakespeare's . . . '

'Why don't . . . why don't you try?' she murmured.

'I can . . . only think of something

162

. . . that isn't very original . . . I love you . . . '

'I'd rather hear you say that,' she answered, 'than any words of Shakespeare's . . . '

\* \* \*

'Keith, it's awfully late,' said Tangye, some time later.

'Yes, darling, I'm afraid it is,' he agreed.

'Tell me something . . . did you *know* Ronnie Hays would be out tonight?'

'Well . . . er . . . '

'Did you?'

'Well, yes . . . er . . . as a matter of fact, I did . . . '

'I ought to be very cross with you . . . '

'But you're not?'

'No. I'm rather glad . . . '

\* \* \*

The taxi ran smoothly down Oxford Street. It was late and there was little traffic. Tangye sat back in sleepy happiness, cradled in the crook of Keith's arm.

'You'll soon be home now, darling,' he said. 'There's the Regency Theatre and — '

He stopped abruptly, leaned suddenly forward and tapped on the window.

'Driver — driver!' he called, sharply. 'Stop . . . stop!'

'What on earth are you doing?' cried Tangye, startled into full wakefulness. 'What's the matter?'

'Didn't you see? Driver — stop!'

'See what?' she demanded as the cab drew in to the kerb.

'There was a light in the theatre,' said Keith. 'Somebody with a torch . . . '

He opened the door as the taxi stopped, and jumped quickly out.

'You go on home, darling,' he said.

'What are you going to do?' she asked.

'I'm going to find out who's in the theatre at this time of night,' he answered.

'Keith, don't go,' she said, earnestly. 'You don't know *what's* there!'

'I mean to find out,' he said.

'Very well,' she said, 'then I'm coming with you.'

He started to protest, but she was out

of the taxi before he could stop her. He dropped some money into the driver's hand and they hurried up the side-turning to the stage door.

'Are you sure the light you saw wasn't just a reflection?' she said.

He shook his head.

'Quite,' he said. 'It was a torch. If anyone had a right to be there they would have put the lights on.'

'How could anyone get in?' she asked.

'We'll soon find out,' said Keith, grimly.

They reached the stage door and he tried the handle. The door opened.

'There you are,' he whispered, excitedly. 'There *is* someone there . . . '

She clutched his arm.

'Don't go in,' Keith,' she implored, 'please don't go in. You don't know *who's* in there.'

'You needn't come,' he said. 'I must go and see.'

'Of course I'm coming,' she answered, 'but do be careful . . . Remember what happened to Alexander Mayne . . . '

'Keep behind me,' he whispered, and gently pushed the door open. When they were inside the passage they stopped to listen. There was no sound.

'Put the lights on, Tangye,' said Keith. 'The switch is just inside the door.'

She felt about in the darkness, found the switch and pressed it down. The light came on and they looked about them. The passage stretched away to the bend — empty.

'Can you hear anything?' he asked.

She listened and shook her head.

'No, not a sound.'

'Let's go through to the stage,' he said.

She followed him down the empty passage. As they passed the locked and sealed door of Castleton Mayne's old dressing room she gave a sudden little shiver. The iron door to the stage was shut and it creaked loudly as Keith opened it. Beyond was complete darkness.

'I can't see a thing,' she whispered.

'You'd better stay where you are until I put on the pilot light,' he said. 'Don't move, darling, or you may fall over something.'

'All right.'

He moved away across the stage,

feeling his way carefully. He found the switchboard and struck a match to find the right switch that would light the single batten light. He found it and pulled it down.

'There,' he said, and his voice echoed in the empty theatre, 'now we can see.' He turned to where the girl should have been, but she was no longer there. 'Tangye,' he called, sharply. 'Tangye, where are you?'

Nobody answered him. Nothing but silence.

'Tangye!' he cried in sudden alarm. 'Tangye, where are you? Tangye — '

This time a voice did answer, but it was not Tangye's. It was a man's voice, resonant and clear. It echoed through the theatre in rolling periods:

''*To be, or not to be, that is the question; whether 'tis nobler in the mind, to suffer the slings and arrows of outrageous fortune, or to take arms against a sea of troubles, and by opposing end them? To die — to sleep . . .* ''

'Who's that?' cried Keith, hoarsely. 'Who's there?'

' . . . 'no more: and, by a sleep, to say we end the heartache and the thousand natural shocks that flesh is heir to — 'tis a consummation devoutly to be wished . . .''

'Stop it!' shouted Keith. 'Stop this stupid nonsense, whoever you are!'

''To die — to sleep . . . To sleep! Perchance to dream; ay, there's the rub; for in that sleep of death what dreams may come . . .''

'Who's there? Who's there?' cried Keith, for the stage was empty. The voice came from nowhere, filling the air. 'Tangye . . . ' He ran, stumbling over to the iron door, gripped by a sudden panic. 'Tangye! Oh, God! What's happened to her . . . '

Down the steps and into the passage, lighted, silent, and deserted.

'Tangye — Tangye . . . Why don't you answer? Where are you? Tangye . . . Tangye . . . Tangye!'

But she wasn't there. She had vanished! Completely and utterly — during the short time it had taken him to walk across the stage to the switchboard.

# 11

Keith stopped at the stage door. What could have happened to the girl? There was now no sound in the theatre. The passage, lit by the naked electric bulbs, showed up cold and empty.

For the first time in his life Keith Gilbert knew what terror was. He was suddenly desperately afraid; a cold, flesh-creeping fear that took away his breath like a plunge into icy water and brought the sweat out in little beads on his forehead.

'Tangye!' he called, frantically. 'Tangye!'

But only the echo of his voice answered.

And then he saw the stage door begin to open slowly. A helmeted head was thrust inside, and a voice said, gruffly:

'What's goin' on 'ere, eh?'

'Have you seen a girl leave here?' asked Keith.

The policeman looked at him suspiciously. 'A girl?' he repeated.

'Yes,' said Keith, impatiently. 'Have you seen her?' The policeman, still regarding him suspiciously, came inside.

'I 'aven't seen anybody,' he answered. 'I found this door open and I heard shoutin' . . . '

'She must be still in the building,' said Keith, and turned.

'Look 'ere,' said the policeman, 'what's all this about, eh? Who's this girl, an' what are you doin' here?'

'I belong to the show that's opening here,' said Keith. 'Don't waste — '

'Oh, you do? What's your name?' demanded the policeman.

'Gilbert — Keith Gilbert. Don't waste time asking silly questions, man. We've got to find Miss Ward. She must be here somewhere — '

'Miss Ward? Is she the girl you was askin' about?'

'Yes, yes, of course she is . . . Will you come and . . . '

'Just a minute.' The policeman was not to be hurried. 'I want to get the 'ang o' this. It may be all right, but it seems queer to me. What was you an' this girl doin' 'ere at this time o' night?'

Keith checked the angry retort that he wanted to make.

'I saw a light in here . . . a torch flickering . . . we came to see what it was . . . '

''Ow did you get in?' said the policeman. 'Did you 'ave a key?'

'No, the stage door was open . . . Look here, we've got to find Miss Ward . . . '

'Now, don't you be in a hurry . . . '

'But it may he serious . . . Don't you understand?'

'You saw a light, yer say?' said the policeman, dealing with one thing at a time. 'Who was in 'ere with a torch?'

'I don't know,' snapped Keith. He was rapidly losing patience. 'The important thing is to find Tangye. Stop wasting time and let's look for her . . . '

'Where 'ave you looked?' asked the policeman.

'I haven't looked anywhere, I haven't had time . . . '

'Surely she'd have 'eard you callin'? I could 'ear you outside . . . '

'She *must* be here,' began Keith, and

stopped. From somewhere round the bend of the passage there came a sound — a faint moan.

'Tangye!' called Keith.

'I'm . . . I'm here . . . ' The voice was very faint, but it was unmistakably Tangye's.

Keith hurried back towards the stage with the policeman at his heels.

'Where are you?' he shouted. 'Tangye, where are you?'

'Here . . . '

Tangye was standing at the top of the steps by the iron door leading to the stage. She was white-faced and dazed, and she swayed a little.

'What happened?' asked Keith, anxiously, slipping his arm round her. 'Where have you been?'

'I was waiting . . . for you . . . to . . . to put . . . the light on,' she explained with difficulty, leaning heavily against him. 'Something hit me . . . My head hurts terribly . . . '

'You look pretty bad, Miss,' broke in the policeman. 'Better sit down for a bit.'

'Sit here — on the steps,' said Keith.

He helped her down and she sat on the top step, leaning against him, with his arm round her.

'It's my head,' she complained, weakly. 'It's . . . dreadfully sore.'

'Let me 'ave a look,' said the policeman. He made a deft and unexpectedly tender examination. 'H'm,' he remarked, 'you've 'ad a nasty bash an' no mistake, Miss.'

'Do you mean somebody hit her?' demanded Keith.

The policeman nodded. There was a suspicious look in his eyes as he regarded Keith.

'That's about the size of it,' he said. 'The skin isn't broke, but there's a nasty lump . . . '

'Did you see anyone?' asked Keith, turning to Tangye.

'No,' she replied, 'I didn't see anything. I was just standing when a dreadful pain suddenly shot through my head and I don't remember anything after that until I found myself lying behind some scenery . . . '

'I didn't see anyone either,' said Keith,

'but whoever it was must be still here — somewhere . . . '

Almost as though it was an answer to what he had just said, a dull thud reached their ears from the direction of the stage door.

'Oh, what was that?' Tangye started violently.

'The stage door,' answered Keith, grimly. 'Somebody's just gone out . . . the person, whoever it was, who hit you on the head . . . '

★   ★   ★

It was late on the following morning. In Angus Macdonald's office a little group of people sat discussing the development of the previous night. Macdonald sat in his usual place behind the big desk. Inspector Hinton occupied the leather chair in front of the desk, and Keith and Tangye sat in the other, she in the chair and he perched on the arm.

'There's no doubt,' said Hinton, 'that somebody *is* in possession of a duplicate key to the stage door of the Regency.

That's obvious now.'

'Why should they want it?' asked Macdonald. 'What purpose could they have for wishing to get into a place like the Regency? There's nothing of value there.'

'I've no idea,' said Hinton. 'You know, in the light of this fresh evidence supplied by Mr. Gilbert and Miss Ward we shall have to reconsider our original theory with regard to the murder of Alexander Mayne.'

'Aye, it's a very queer affair, Inspector,' said Macdonald. 'There's no reasonable explanation for all these things that keep happening.'

Hinton examined the tips of his fingers.

'It looks to me,' he remarked, after a slight pause, 'as if the re-opening of the theatre had interfered with somebody's plan — what plan I can't tell you. That message on the door of your flat — I wish you'd told me about that before, Mr. Gilbert — and all these other things seem to suggest that someone is trying to scare you . . . '

'Make us give up the Regency, you

mean?' asked Keith.

Hinton nodded.

'But why?' asked Tangye.

'I'd very much like to know that myself,' he answered.

'The only person I can think of who'd like to scare ye away from the Regency is — Isobel Mayne,' said Macdonald.

'I've considered her,' said Hinton. 'She's in a position to have a duplicate key, too.'

'But . . . but she wouldn't have killed her own son, surely?' said Tangye.

'I wouldn't like to swear to that, Miss Ward,' said Hinton.

'Oh, no.' She shivered. 'It's a horrible idea.'

'You can never tell what a person in her unbalanced state of mind might do,' he said. 'She was very upset that her son let you have the theatre, wasn't she?'

'Yes, and she warned us that there was danger and death there,' said Macdonald, 'but I canna think that she'd go as far as murder. How could she? She's only able to walk with the help of a stick.'

'That's true,' agreed Hinton. He looked

from one to the other for a moment in silence and then he added: 'Did you know the stick she uses is a sword-stick?'

'A sword-stick?' repeated Tangye.

'Yes, it belonged to her husband.'

'But Mayne was killed with that knife . . . ' began Macdonald.

'We can't be sure of that.'

'It wasn't a woman's voice I heard last night in the Regency,' put in Keith.

'Ah, now — I was coming to that,' said Hinton. 'This voice — it was reciting a speech from *Hamlet*, you say?'

'Yes.'

'I'm glad I never heard it,' said Tangye. 'I should have been scared to death.'

'It scared *me*,' admitted Keith.

'What was it like? What kind of voice?' asked Hinton.

'It was a man's voice — an actor's voice,' answered Keith. 'The speech was beautifully delivered . . . '

'Where did it seem to come from?'

'It seemed to fill the whole place,' said Keith. 'That was probably due to the echo . . . '

'Would you say,' asked Hinton, 'that

this 'voice' bore any resemblance to Castleton Mayne's?'

'I couldn't tell you,' replied Keith. 'He was before my time, Inspector.'

'Ye're no suggestin' that there was something supernatural about it?' said Macdonald.

Hinton shrugged his shoulders slightly.

'No,' he said, 'but there's been a lot of Castleton Mayne about this business and I was just wondering . . . You never *saw* anybody, Mr. Gilbert?'

'No.'

'Nor you, Miss Ward?'

She shook her head.

'No,' she answered. 'It was just as if the roof had fallen on me.'

'The person who attacked you must have been hiding just by the door leading to the stage,' remarked Hinton, thoughtfully. 'When Mr. Gilbert put on the light you would have seen who it was so they . . . '

He broke off as there came a tap on the door and Olivia Winter came in. She put a sheaf of papers on the desk in front of Macdonald.

'Here are the contracts you asked for, Mr. Macdonald,' she said.

As she was going out again, Hinton called her. 'Oh, Miss Winter,' he said.

She stopped, her hand on the door handle.

'You remember telling me about the man who came to this office and left that knife,' he said. 'On the day of the murder . . . '

'It was no man,' she replied. 'Men can't make themselves invisible — not while they're alive.'

She was quite serious. Hinton raised his eyebrows.

'I see you're quite convinced it was a ghost,' he said. 'But there was nothing ghostly about the knife, was there? That was real enough. I've got it at the Yard now . . . '

'That was real enough,' she agreed.

'What I wanted to ask you,' he went on, 'is whether this man could have been 'made up' in any way?'

'He wasn't,' she declared with conviction.

'You're quite sure of that?'

'Quite sure,' she said.

'Thank you,' he said. 'That is all I wanted to ask you, Miss Winter.'

She nodded and went out. Hinton rose to his feet and took his hat from the desk.

'I won't bother you any more for the present,' he said. 'I'll just go round and have a word with Mrs. Isobel Mayne, I think . . . '

'Don't you think,' said Keith, 'that we ought to have a new lock put on the stage door of the theatre?'

Hinton rubbed his chin thoughtfully. Then he shook his head.

'No,' he said, 'I don't think I would. It would be a pity to keep this intruder out. The next time he comes we might catch him . . . '

⋆ ⋆ ⋆

Mrs. Isobel Mayne surveyed Inspector Hinton coldly, though somewhere behind the deep-set eyes lurked a wary expression.

'I told you before,' she said, 'that it is useless asking me questions. I can tell you nothing — nothing. You are only wasting your time.'

'Surely you are as anxious as we are to find the person or persons who killed your son, Mrs. Mayne?' he said.

'My son was not killed by a person,' she retorted, 'unless the evil gathered in that old building assumed a human shape for its purpose. I warned Alexander what would happen if he tampered with things he did not understand . . . '

'So I've heard,' said Hinton. 'How did you know *anything* would happen?'

'Because it happened before,' she answered, simply. 'The same evil that killed my husband is still there . . . '

'Your husband was killed by a man called Marsden,' he said, quickly.

'Marsden?' She laughed scornfully. 'He was only the instrument. When it had used him the evil sent him mad and he died. But the evil continued . . . '

'You had no other reason for believing that something would happen if the Regency was re-opened?' Hinton persisted.

'What other reason is necessary?' she

said. 'Isn't it enough? Hasn't it proved to be true?'

'Well, I suppose it has, in a way,' he admitted. 'Before your son opened the theatre, Mrs. Mayne, somebody had been there — quite a number of times — are you sure there are no other keys?'

The mask of cold calm cracked. A spasm of anger twisted her mouth, and the old eyes sparkled with sudden fire.

'Stop!' she cried, in a voice that was hoarse and rasping. 'Stop! I will answer no more questions. What is the use? There are things you don't understand — things you will never understand . . .'

'I'm trying to understand, Mrs. Mayne,' he broke in, gently. 'Somebody is still using the Regency Theatre for some purpose — somebody who has no right there. They were there again last night. A girl was attacked . . .'

'The fools!' she burst out, angrily. 'The fools! Why don't they go? I warned them — could I do more? Why don't they leave the place and shut it up again? That is the only way . . . there will be nothing but trouble until they do . . .'

'Why?' said Hinton. 'Tell me *why*, Mrs. Mayne.'

'Go away and leave me alone,' she said. 'You won't believe what I tell you. You think I don't know what I'm talking about, don't you? But I do . . . You're all blind — blind . . . '

The door opened and Mrs. Duppy came in anxiously.

'Did you call, dearie?' she asked.

'Duppy — take this man away,' ordered her mistress. 'Take him away. I can't stand any more . . . '

The old woman looked at Hinton venomously.

'Have you been upsetting her?' she snapped.

'I've only been asking a few questions,' he said.

'Why can't you leave her alone?' demanded Mrs. Duppy. 'Hasn't she had enough trouble without you pestering her with questions? She can't help you, and it only makes her bad . . . '

'Go away,' said Mrs. Mayne. 'Go away . . . '

Hinton realized that it was useless

staying. He would get nothing further out of either of them — even if they knew anything.

'Mrs. Duppy,' he said on the way downstairs, 'perhaps you can help me. Are there any other keys to the Regency Theatre besides those Mr. Mayne had?'

'I don't know,' she answered. 'There are no keys here.'

'Does Mrs. Mayne go out at all — by herself?' he asked.

'Sometimes,' she said. 'Not often — she's not very strong. I nearly always go with her.'

'But not always?'

'No, not always. Sometimes she takes a little walk in the afternoon.'

'Have you ever known her to go out at — night?'

'Good gracious, what a thing to ask,' she said. 'Of course not.'

'Would you know if she did?' he asked.

'She doesn't,' said the old woman. 'What would she want to go out at night for?'

Hinton made no reply. They had reached the front door, and she was standing with it open in her hand.

'Good-bye,' he said. 'I'm sorry to have had to bother you again.'

She shut the door behind him, stood for a minute in the hall, and then walked slowly back up the stairs. Mrs. Mayne met her on the landing.

'You didn't tell him anything, Duppy?' she inquired, eagerly.

'No, dearie, no,' said Mrs. Duppy, soothingly. 'Don't worry yourself . . . '

'That's right, Duppy,' Mrs. Mayne chuckled. 'They mustn't find out, must they? They mustn't find out . . . *Where did you hide the key, Duppy?*'

# 12

'Have some more coffee, Tangye?' said Maysie Sheringham. 'We've got plenty of time.'

'I don't want any more,' said Tangye. 'You have some, though.'

'I think I will.' Maysie called the waitress and gave her order. 'I told you that Lemoine model would do the trick, didn't I?'

Tangye laughed.

'I don't think it was entirely the dress,' she said.

'Well, no — perhaps not entirely,' agreed Maysie. 'I expect you had *something* to do with it, darling. I'm glad for you.'

'Thank you.'

'How's your head?'

'It's still a little sore . . . '

'Not the ideal ending to an evening of romance,' said Maysie, and then seriously: 'I wonder what can be going on in that theatre?'

'I don't know . . . '

'You wouldn't get me in there alone for all the tea in China,' declared Maysie, emphatically. 'You've no idea who hit you?'

'No — I didn't see anyone . . . '

'Well, I wish I knew what was going on,' said Maysie. 'There's . . . Oh, look, here's Victor.'

Victor Price saw them and came over to the table.

'Hello, girls,' he said. 'D'you mind if I sit here? All the other tables are full . . . '

'We'll be going in a minute,' said Maysie. 'We've had our lunch.'

He sat down.

'How did you get on at the dressmaker's?' he asked. 'Were the dresses all right?'

'All except two,' said Maysie. 'They're making some alterations to those. I've got to go back this afternoon.'

'What are they like?'

'Oh, they're lovely,' she said, enthusiastically.

'All mine have to be altered,' put in

Tangye. 'I'm not as big as Madeleine Peters . . .'

'How are you feeling now?' asked Price.

'My head's a bit painful, but otherwise I feel all right.'

'That must have been a nasty crack you got,' he remarked.

'It was.'

'I can't understand it at all.' He shook his head. 'What do you think is going on?'

'If anyone else asks me that, I shall scream,' declared Tangye.

'Oh, I'm sorry . . .'

'It's all right, Victor. But I think everybody in the theatre has asked me that. I don't know what's going on — I didn't see anything or anyone.'

'It's damned queer,' said Price, 'all these things that keep cropping up. You never know what's going to happen next . . .'

'You're telling us,' said Maysie. 'The only good thing is that your dress wasn't ruined, Tangye.'

'You were lucky,' said Price. 'Pale lilac shows every mark.'

'It got a bit dusty, but it brushed off,' said Tangye.

'Look, I must go.' Maysie got up. 'I've got to be at the dressmaker's in five minutes . . . '

'I'll come with you,' said Tangye. 'Will you explain to Mr. Brett, Victor? We'll get back to rehearsal as soon as we can . . . '

'I'll tell him,' said Price. 'Cheerio!'

When they reached the street, Tangye said, suddenly:

'Maysie, it's just struck me . . . How did Victor *know* that I was wearing a lilac-coloured dress last night?'

★ ★ ★

There was a tap at the door of Inspector Hinton's cheerless little office at Scotland Yard, and, in answer to his 'Come in' the door opened and Sergeant Boler entered. He was a large man with a florid face and thinning hair.

'You sent for me, sir?' he said, respectfully.

'Yes, Boler. Sit down,' said Hinton.

189

The Detective-Sergeant perched himself on the edge of a chair.

'Look, I'll tell you what I want you to do,' said Hinton. He picked up a paper from his desk and held it out. 'Here's a list of all the people connected with this Regency Theatre business. I want you to check up on them — where they come from, who their relations are, everything that you can find out about 'em — understand?'

'Yes, sir,' said Boler. He glanced at the list. 'It's going to be rather a long job.'

'I may be able to shorten it for you,' said Hinton. 'Do you see the name that I've ringed round in red?'

'Yes, sir.'

'If you start with that person you may not have to bother with any of the others.'

Boler looked at him. There was a startled expression in his large eyes.

'You mean . . . this is the person who killed Mayne?' he asked.

'I don't know,' said Hinton, 'but, from something that occurred, I've an idea it *might* be . . . '

Madeleine Peters, clad in a very becoming housecoat of pale blue velvet trimmed with cherry-coloured silk, lay on the settee in her flat idly listening to the radio. A fashion magazine was half open on the floor where she had dropped it when the contents had begun to bore her.

There was a ring at the front doorbell, and getting up she switched off the radio and went to admit the expected visitor.

'Come in, Phillip,' she said.

Defoe took off his hat and coat, threw them on to an oak chest, and followed her into the sitting room.

'You are alone?' he asked, abruptly. 'You sent your maid out as I told you?'

'Yes . . .'

'Good.' He put down a parcel he was carrying, and she eyed it curiously.

'Why were you so insistent that I should get rid of Anna?' she asked.

'I wish to talk to you,' he answered, 'and I don't want anyone to overhear.'

'You're being very mysterious, aren't you?' she said. 'You've often talked to

191

me before, without worrying about Anna . . . '

'This is different,' he said.

'Apparently.' She shrugged her shoulders. 'Well, sit down. Would you like a drink?'

'Please . . . some whisky.' Defoe dropped into a chair and crossed his legs. Madeleine went over to a cocktail cabinet and poured out a John Haig.

'What have you got in that parcel?' she asked. 'A present?'

'You — could call it that,' he answered with a smile.

'For me?'

'No, not for you, Madeleine. That is what is going to stop our friend Brett from opening at the Regency.'

'Oh,' she said, coming over with the whisky, and perching on the arm of his chair. 'You got it then?'

'It was finished this afternoon.' He took the glass from her and drank some of the contents.

She nodded.

'I understand, now, why you wanted to get rid of Anna,' she said.

'I don't think you do,' he said, 'not entirely . . . '

'What do you mean?' she said, quickly.

'Well, you see, my dear,' — he looked up at her — 'you are going to do this . . . '

She jumped up as though she had been stung.

'No, Phillip, no . . . I won't!'

'Come now,' he said softly, 'you're not going to spoil everything by being silly . . . '

'I'm not being silly. Why should I do it? Why can't you do it?'

'Because, my dear,' said Defoe, and his voice was silky, 'in case there should be any suspicion against me, I wish to provide myself with an alibi. When I leave here I shall drive down to some friends of mine in the country. I shall stay there until the morning . . . '

'What about me?' she demanded. 'Supposing I'm suspected?'

'Nobody will suspect you, my dear.'

'I won't do it!' she declared. 'I mean it, Phillip. I won't do it.'

'But it's all so quick and simple,' he said, persuasively. 'Look, here is the key.

It is only a matter of two — three — four minutes at the outside . . . '

She ignored the key he held out.

'No,' she said.

He got up slowly, like the uncoiling of a snake preparing to strike.

'Madeleine,' he said, and there was something of the hiss of a snake in his voice, 'you do not wish to make me angry . . . do you?'

'I don't care whether you're angry or not,' she snapped.

'I think you would care . . . if I really lost my temper,' he said.

She tried to stare at him defiantly, but her eyes dropped.

'Phillip,' she entreated, 'please don't make me do it . . . '

'I am being very patient, Madeleine,' he said coldly, 'but my patience is not inexhaustible. I have explained to you why it is necessary for you to do this . . . '

'Supposing . . . I make a mess of it?'

'You will not do that for your own sake,' he said.

'I'm scared,' she said. 'I tell you I'm scared . . . '

'Don't be a fool!' he said, impatiently. 'There's nothing to get scared about. It is quite a simple thing that I'm asking you to do . . . '

'Simple!' she scoffed. 'You're asking me to take all the risk. If anything goes wrong I shall bear the full brunt of it . . . '

'Nothing will go wrong, unless you lose your head and do something stupid. You yourself said the scheme was fool-proof . . . '

'I never thought that you were going to make me carry it out,' she retorted.

'All you have to do is to open a door, for which I have provided a key, leave that parcel behind you, and come away. What could be easier?'

'When do you want me to go?' she asked, wearily.

'About nine o'clock,' he answered. 'You must be careful to see that there is no one about . . . '

'Don't worry . . . I shall . . . All right, I'll go . . . '

'I am glad you are being reasonable, my dear,' he said. 'It would be a pity if we quarrelled over such a stupid thing . . . '

'There are times, Phillip,' she said bitterly, 'when I think I hate you . . . '

'You don't mean that,' he said. 'You get nervy and say these things.'

'Do I?'

He came to her and took her in his arms.

'I will show you,' he whispered, 'that you do not hate me . . . '

Bending his head he kissed her. She stood stiffly unresponsive for a moment, and then she yielded . . .

★　★　★

Ronnie Hays whistled softly as he typed busily. He was alone in the flat and working on the new sketch to fill the gap in the second half of the show. The ringing of the front doorbell interrupted him, and with a muttered 'blast!' he got up and went to see who was disturbing his labours. It was Clifford Brett and Nutty.

'Hello,' said Brett. 'Is Keith in?'

Hays shook his head.

'He's taken Tangye out somewhere,' he

said. 'Sit down . . . There are some cigarettes over on that table . . . Help yourselves. I'll get you a drink. What would you like?'

'Beer for me,' said Nutty.

'Whisky for me, if there is any,' said Brett.

'I think there's half a bottle of Haig here somewhere,' said Hays, opening the sideboard cupboard. 'Yes, here we are.'

He poured out the drinks.

'I hope we're not disturbing your work?' said Brett.

'No, I'm nearly finished . . . Here you are, Nutty . . .'

Nutty took the glass of beer he held out.

'We wondered,' Brett continued, 'if you felt like a spot of adventure?'

'What do you mean? What sort of adventure?' asked Hays.

'Well, that depends — it might be quite exciting . . .'

'We're goin' ter 'ave a bash at solvin' the mystery o' the Regency Theatre,' said Nutty over the top of his beer glass.

'What on earth are you talking about?'

Hays handed Brett a glass of whisky.

'You ask Mr. Brett — 'e'll tell yer,' said Nutty.

'You know what happened to Tangye and Keith, Ronnie!' said Brett. 'Somebody seems to be making pretty free with the place and prowling about there at night whenever the fancy takes 'em. Nutty and I thought it would be a good idea to lie in wait and find out who it is.'

'It's a good idea,' said Ronnie. 'You can count on me.'

'Good. I should think if we got to the theatre about ten it would be time enough. I don't suppose this prowler starts his tricks too early.'

'The thing that puzzles me,' said Hays, pouring himself a whisky and soda, 'is why he starts 'em at all. Why on earth should anyone want to wander about a theatre in the middle of the night?'

'Spoutin' bits o' Shakespeare,' said Nutty. 'Lumme . . . if I'd been Mr. Gilbert I'd 'ave 'ad the breeze up proper.'

'You'd better not come with us tonight then, Nutty,' said Brett, laughing. 'There may be some more of it.'

'Oh, that's different,' declared the little man. 'We'll be expectin' it like, won't we?'

'Perhaps he doesn't perform every night,' said Hays. 'You know, I would like to get to the bottom of this business.'

'Blimey, so would I,' declared Nutty. 'There must be a blinkin' reason be'ind it all.'

'Unless we're all wrong and Isobel Mayne is right,' said Brett.

'That there's something — evil about the place, you mean?'

Brett nodded.

'Lumme,' exclaimed Nutty, 'you're not goin' over ter the spooks, are yer?'

'No, of course not,' said Brett.

'That business of the knife was queer, you know,' remarked Hays, thoughtfully.

'I think the man was made up to look like Castleton Mayne,' said Brett, 'the same as that message on your door was made to look like Mayne's handwriting.'

'How did he get in and out of the office without being seen by the lift man?'

'Well, he could have come in much earlier and waited in one of the upper corridors,' answered Brett. 'However it was managed, I'm quite sure it was all part of the plan to try and scare us out of the theatre.'

'But why?' demanded Ronnie Hays. 'What for?'

'Now we're back to Miss 'Ay again,' put in Nutty, grinning. 'Blimey, this is more like 'Twenty Questions' than 'Ignorance is Bliss', ain't it?'

'A bit of both is more like it, Nutty,' said Brett. He finished his whisky. 'We'll get starting in a minute or two . . . '

'I've got my old army revolver in the bedroom,' said Hays. 'Shall I bring it? There are a few rounds of ammo, I think . . . '

'You might as well, Ronnie,' said Brett. 'After all, we don't know what we're likely to come up against tonight, do we?'

# 13

It was very dark and still inside the Regency Theatre. Behind a stack of scenery that leaned against the wall near the prompt corner, Brett, Nutty, and Ronnie Hays crouched waiting. The darkness all round them was so intense that it felt like something solid — a wall that was pressing in upon them. Faintly from somewhere outside a clock struck the half-hour.

'Blimey,' breathed Nutty, shifting his cramped legs, ''alf-past eleven. We've been 'ere nearly a blinkin' hour and a quarter . . . '

'Don't get impatient,' whispered Brett.

'Could we hear from here if anyone comes in the stage door?' asked Hays, under his breath.

'Yes, I think so,' answered Brett. 'This empty place acts like a sounding board. We ought to hear quite clearly.'

'Lumme, I could do with a smoke,' said

Nutty, longingly.

'I'm afraid you'll just have to go without,' said Brett. 'It would give our presence away if the intruder smelt tobacco . . . '

'It's like waiting for zero hour, isn't it?' said Hays.

'Yes, do you remember that night in the desert, Ronnie? We were going to attack at dawn, and while we were waiting for the signal somebody fired a Verey pistol and we suddenly saw hordes of Jerries looming out of the darkness, almost on top of our lines . . . '

'Yes!' said Ronnie. 'That was a near thing . . . '

'We never found out who was the genius who fired the Verey light, but it saved our bacon . . . '

'Sh-s-s!' broke in Nutty, warningly. 'Quiet! I 'eard somethink.'

They listened with straining ears.

Silence!

'You must have made a mistake, Nutty,' began Brett.

'I can hear it too,' said Hays. 'Somebody's just come in the stage door . . . '

They all heard it now — a faint click

and a soft thud. The closing of the door. There was a short interval of complete silence, and then they heard the sound of a stealthy step coming along the passage.

'Let him get well on to the stage,' whispered Brett, with his lips close to Ronnie's ear, 'and then when I give the word, put on the light. Nutty and I will tackle him.'

Hays nodded.

The footsteps, barely audible, were coming nearer. They came up the steps outside the iron door and on to the stage. They paused and then began to walk slowly across the bare boards . . .

'Now!' cried Brett, suddenly. Hays sprang up and pulled down the switch controlling the pilot light. It lit the big stage faintly, but it was sufficient to see Brett and Nutty struggling with someone in the middle.

'All right, I've got 'im!' panted Nutty. 'Now then, let's 'ave a look at yer . . . '

'Good Lord!' exclaimed Brett as he caught sight of the face of the man they had captured. 'It's Inspector Hinton!'

Hinton was almost as surprised.

'Mr. Brett!' he exclaimed.

'Cor blimey!' grunted Nutty, disgustedly. 'I thought we'd got 'im.'

Hinton smoothed his hair and straightened his tie.

'It looks as if we'd all had the same idea,' he said.

Brett grinned ruefully.

'It does, doesn't it?' he said.

'I was hoping there might be another visit tonight,' said Hinton. 'How long have you been here?'

'Since ten o'clock,' answered Brett. 'Look here, how did you get in?'

'That wasn't very difficult,' said Hinton. 'I've a key . . . '

'A key?' said Hays. 'How did you get . . . ?'

'One of my men took an impression of the lock, and I had a key cut,' explained Hinton. 'I could get into a row at headquarters if you like to make a fuss about it . . . '

'You needn't worry about that,' said Brett. 'You could have saved yourself a lot of trouble, though, if you'd just asked me.'

'I had reasons for not wanting you or anybody else to know,' said Hinton. 'Do you mind if we put that light out? If somebody *is* contemplating a visit, that'll scare 'em off . . . '

Hays started to walk over to the switchboard when they heard a faint thud from the passage beyond the iron door.

'Did you 'ear that?' whispered Nutty.

'Yes, what was it?' asked Brett.

'Something out in the passage,' said Hays.

'Come on, let's see,' snapped Hinton.

He hurried over to the iron door and down the steps into the passage, with the others at his heels.

'Put a light on here — quickly,' he ordered.

Brett found the switch and pressed it down. Light flooded the passage from end to end, but it was deserted.

'There's nobody here,' said Hinton. 'I wonder what the hell that noise was . . . '

'Look,' cried Nutty, and there was horror in his voice. 'Look there . . . Cor blimey, look . . . '

'What's the matter?' asked Brett, sharply.

'Can't yer see it?' said Nutty. 'On the floor there . . . comin' from under the door of the sealed dressin' room.'

They all saw it now. A thin, sluggish stream that was slowly spreading . . .

'My God!' muttered Clifford Brett, incredulously. 'It's blood!'

There was no doubt. It *was* blood. An irregular pool had formed on the floor and it was flooding from under the door. In the overhead lights of the passage it glistened redly . . .

Hinton went over and, stooping, touched it with his finger.

'It's incredible,' he muttered.

'It's impossible,' declared Hays, 'the door's locked and sealed . . . '

'And it hasn't been opened.' Hinton examined the seals. 'These haven't been disturbed for years . . . '

''Ow did that get there then?' asked Nutty, pointing at the red pool.

'There must be another way into the room,' said Brett. 'What about the window?'

'Shuttered and screwed up from the inside,' said Hinton. 'I examined the outside myself at the time Alexander Mayne was killed.'

'But this is *wet*,' said Hays. '*Wet* . . . '

'Yes, we shall have to break the door down,' said Hinton.

'What about the clause in our agree — '

'Can't help that, Mr. Brett,' snapped Hinton. 'I'll take the responsibility. There's someone in there who is in a pretty bad way by the look of it — possibly dead . . . '

'There's a fireman's axe by the hydrant on the stage,' said Brett. 'That 'ud do the trick . . . '

'I'll fetch it,' said Hays. He hurried away.

'Who can it be in there?' asked Nutty.

'Heaven knows — or how they got in,' said Brett.

'We'll soon find out who it is,' said Hinton.

After a few minutes Hays came back with a wicked-looking axe.

'Here you are,' he said.

Hinton took it and attacked the door.

The wood was tough and well-seasoned. At first the axe made little impression, but he stuck at it and presently the door began to give.

'Another second 'ull do it,' he panted.

The door suddenly swung inwards a few inches and stopped.

'That's got it,' said Hinton, and gave the door a shove. 'Hello, there's still something stopping it from opening fully . . . '

'I can squeeze through,' said Nutty. He edged his small body round the partly open door. 'Lumme, it's dark. Yer can't see nothink . . . '

'If it's like the other dressing rooms there's a switch just inside the door,' said Brett.

'I don't suppose there's a bulb,' began Ronnie.

'We'll soon see,' muttered Nutty. He felt about in the dark and a light came on. 'There yer are,' he said triumphantly, and then: 'Cor blimey! There's a woman . . . lynin' on the floor . . . '

'A woman!' exclaimed Hinton.

'Yes, that's what was stoppin' the door from openin',' said Nutty. 'Oh, my Gawd

. . . it's Madeleine Peters!'

'Madeleine Peters!' echoed Brett, incredulously.

'Is she . . . is she dead?' asked Ronnie Hays.

'Yes, I'm afraid so,' answered Hinton. 'Look at her throat. She was killed the same way that Alexander Mayne was killed . . . '

'Oh, look!' There was sheer horror in Nutty's voice. 'Look . . . over there . . . sittin' in the chair by the mirror . . . Strewth! *What is it?*'

They looked, and Brett felt his flesh creep and the hairs of his neck stir. Seated by the dressing table on which were still set out the sticks of grease paint, the pots of cream, and make-up materials he had used in life, was a black-clad figure.

'God!' breathed Brett. 'It's horrible . . . horrible!'

'Who is it?' whispered Hinton. '*Who is it?*'

'Castleton Mayne,' answered Clifford Brett. 'Castleton Mayne — made up and dressed in the clothes he wore as Hamlet . . . '

# 14

'Well, Doctor?' said Hinton.

It was nearly an hour later. The police photographers had been and the finger-print experts had made a thorough examination of the sealed dressing room. They found no other prints except those of Madeleine Peters. These were on the inside of the door and near the light switch. How she had got into the room was a complete mystery; so was the fact that on the dressing table, before the shrivelled body of Castleton Mayne, were fresh flowers.

Doctor Vines, the police surgeon, who had been late in arriving, looked up from his examination when Hinton put his question.

'The woman was killed with a sharp instrument that severed the jugular vein,' he said.

'It would have been a fairly quick death, I suppose?' asked the Inspector.

The doctor nodded.

'Oh, yes — very,' he said. 'A matter of a few seconds only . . . '

'What about the — the other body?' said Hinton.

'That's different,' answered Vines. He went over to the horrible thing in the chair. 'I don't think I've ever come across anything like this before . . . '

'He was killed over thirty years ago,' said Hinton. 'How is it the body's in such a good state of preservation?'

'Some form of embalming process,' replied the doctor. 'It's been pumped full of formaldehyde or something similar. It's very shrunken. The face looks all right because it's been made up . . . '

'That must have been Mrs. Mayne's idea,' said Brett.

Hinton nodded.

'We know now why she wanted this room kept sealed,' he said.

Nutty shivered.

'It's an 'orrible idea, ain't it?' he said. 'Cor lumme — an' them flowers . . . '

'She isn't normal,' said Hinton. 'What

211

puzzles me is how this woman, Peters, got in here.'

'And how her murderer got in — and out,' said Brett.

'There must be another way in,' said Hays.

Hinton shook his head.

'There isn't,' he declared. 'There's only the door.'

'But it's been locked and sealed for thirty years,' said Brett. 'It was still locked and the seals intact when we broke it open ...'

'I know, I know,' broke in Hinton with a wry smile. 'You needn't make it more difficult.'

'He isn't making it difficult, Hinton,' said Doctor Vines, grimly. 'He's making it impossible.'

'It can't be impossible because it happened,' said the Inspector.

'Well, I'll leave you to work it out,' said Vines. 'I've got a heavy day tomorrow and I'm going home to get some sleep. Good night.'

They wished him 'good night' and he took his departure. When he had gone they adjourned to one of the other dressing rooms, leaving a constable on guard in the other. A question which had been worrying Brett he put into words:

'What was Madeleine Peters doing here at all?' he asked.

'I'll bet whatever it was, she was up ter no good,' said Nutty.

'You say, she used to be in the show?' said Hinton.

'Yes, she was our leading lady, but she had a row with Gilbert and walked out. That's how we lost the Rialto Theatre . . . '

'I see.' Hinton rubbed his chin. 'Well, she couldn't be the person we *thought* might come tonight — *that* was the murderer . . . '

'When could it have happened?' asked Ronnie. 'We were here just after ten . . . '

'It must have been before that,' said Hinton. 'She'd been dead for some time . . . You didn't put the light on in the passage when you came in, did you?'

'No, we didn't want to advertise our presence to anyone who might be about.'

'Well, then . . . you wouldn't have seen

the blood — in the dark.'

'Lumme!' breathed Nutty. 'She was in there . . . dead . . . all the time?'

'Yes, she must have been . . . '

'What was the noise we heard . . . like a thud?' said Brett.

'At a guess I'd say it was the body falling against the door,' said Hinton. 'Of course, I don't know. I'm only judging from appearances. There're marks on the wall that look as though it had been propped up at one side of the door . . . '

'What do you think is behind all this, Inspector?' asked Brett.

'Quite frankly, I haven't the least idea,' confessed Hinton. 'But people don't commit murder for nothing — at least not *this* type of murder . . . '

'It's got something to do with the theatre,' said Brett. 'But what on earth could it be?'

'If yer ask me,' broke in Nutty, 'the old lady's at the bottom of it. She didn't want nobody ter know about 'er 'usband bein' 'ere . . . '

'That's why she was so anxious to keep the dressing room locked up —

yes,' answered Hinton. 'But I don't think she hit Miss Ward last night, and it certainly wasn't her voice that Mr. Gilbert heard.'

'Isobel Mayne couldn't have done all these things, Nutty,' said Brett. 'She's over seventy . . . '

'Besides,' put in Ronnie Hays, 'somebody was using this theatre for some purpose of their own long before we ever thought of re-opening it. Isn't that right, Inspector?'

Hinton nodded.

'Well, why couldn't that be 'er?' demanded Nutty. 'Poppin' in ter see that nobody 'ad disturbed . . . what she knew was in that room.'

'It *could* be,' agreed Hinton, doubtfully.

'I say,' said Hays suddenly, 'what about the man who came to Macdonald's office and left the knife . . . ?'

'The man who looked like Castleton Mayne . . . yes,' murmured the Inspector.

'*That* was almost as impossible as getting in and out of that sealed and locked dressing room,' said Brett.

Hinton sighed. He looked tired.

'There's a lot we've got to explain,' he said, wearily.

'Perhaps Phillip Defoe could help you?' suggested Brett.

'Who's he?'

'Madeleine Peters was — well, they were — er — very good friends, if you understand what I mean?'

'I think I do,' said Hinton.

'He might be able to explain what she was doing here tonight,' said Brett.

'Thanks for the tip,' said Hinton. 'I'll make a point of seeing him . . . '

'An' don't ferget to ask 'im about that there key,' said Nutty.

'Key — what key?' said Brett, quickly.

'Lumme, didn't Mr. Hays tell yer . . . ?'

'Oh, Lord, I forgot all about it,' said Ronnie.

'What is this about a key?' snapped Hinton.

'Defoe 'ad one cut at a shop near the Elephant . . . very secret 'e was about it . . . ' Nutty explained.

'I'll certainly look into it,' declared Hinton. 'If that key was the key of the stage door it would account for the way this woman Peters got in.' He yawned. 'Well, I don't think we can do any more here.'

Clifford Brett suddenly thought of the morning rehearsal.

'I suppose we'll be able to rehearse here tomorrow?' he said.

'Oh, yes.' said Hinton. 'We'll screen off the dressing room . . . '

'What will you do with — with Castleton Mayne?' asked Hays.

'We shall take him to the mortuary with the body of Peters,' answered the Inspector. He sighed again. 'I shall have to see Mrs. Mayne. There are a lot of questions she'll *have* to answer now . . . '

'I don't envy you your job,' said Brett.

'Blimey, nor me neither,' declared Nutty.

'Can't say I'm looking forward to it myself,' said Hinton. 'But there's one thing I'm hoping she'll be able to tell me . . . '

'What's that?' asked Brett, as he paused.

'How Madeleine Peters and the murderer got into that locked room *without* disturbing the seals,' said Hinton.

★  ★  ★

The first thing that Detective-Inspector Hinton did on the following morning was to pay his promised visit to Phillip Defoe. It was early when he rang the bell of the flat, and there was an appreciable delay before he got any answer. Then the door was opened by Defoe, himself, in a brightly coloured silk dressing gown.

'What is it?' he asked, ungraciously.

'Mr. Phillip Defoe?' asked Hinton.

'Yes,' answered the other. 'What do you want?'

'I'm Detective-Inspector Hinton of Scotland Yard, sir,' said Hinton, producing his warrant card. 'May I have a word with you?'

'With me?' said Defoe, in apparent surprise. 'What about?'

'I should prefer not to talk about it here. May I come inside?'

'Yes . . . yes, of course.' Defoe led the way into the sitting room. 'Now, what's all this about?'

'It concerns a lady — a Miss Madeleine Peters.'

'Madeleine?' Defoe's eyes were suddenly wary.

'I understand that she was a friend of yours?'

'That is — correct . . . Why are you asking these questions?'

'When did you last see her?' asked Hinton.

'I do not see that it can be any concern of yours — er — Inspector,' said Defoe.

'It happens to be very much my concern,' retorted Hinton. 'She was found dead last night . . . '

Defoe almost staggered. It was like the result of a physical blow. His face went white and he stared at Hinton as though he were a ghost.

'What?' he muttered, huskily. 'What's this you say?'

'Miss Peters was murdered last night,' said Hinton.

'Murdered?' Defoe repeated the word

in a dazed way. 'But ... but it's impossible ... '

'I'm afraid it's true,' said Hinton.

'How did it happen?' demanded Defoe. 'Where ... ?'

'She was found in the Regency Theatre ... '

'The Regency?'

'Yes. There was a wound in her throat ... We've reason to believe that she was killed by the same person, or persons, who killed Alexander Mayne.'

Defoe licked his lips, which seemed to have suddenly gone dry. He went over to the sideboard, opened a cupboard, and took out a bottle of John Haig.

'Do you mind if I have a drink?' he asked, huskily. 'This ... this has been rather a shock ... '

'I can understand that,' said Hinton.

'Perhaps you'd like to join me?' said Defoe.

'No, thank you.'

Defoe poured out a stiff whisky and gulped it down. He was obviously shaken, but the spirit brought a tinge of colour back to his sallow cheeks.

'Ah, that's better,' he said. 'I needed that . . . '

'Now,' said Hinton, 'when did you last see Miss Peters?'

'Yesterday.'

'At what time?'

'Let me see.' Defoe pretended to think. 'It was about half-past seven in the evening, I think.'

'What time did you leave her?'

'Just before eight.'

'During the time she was with you did she mention anything about going to the Regency Theatre for any purpose?'

'No . . . no, I cannot understand why she should have gone there.'

'You didn't give her a key to the stage door?' Defoe was obviously disconcerted by the question. His hand went up to his lips and he fingered them nervously.

'A key? What would I be doing with a key to the stage door of the Regency Theatre?'

'I was wondering if you would tell me that,' said Hinton, quietly.

'I don't understand . . . '

'Did you give Miss Peters a key?'

'No . . . no, of course I didn't!'

'You had a key cut at a small shop near the Elephant and Castle. What was that key for, sir?'

'Oh, that.' Defoe tried to pull himself together. 'Well, that was . . . that was the key to the store cupboard . . . the Rialto. The original key . . . got lost and . . . I had to have another cut.'

'Rather a long way for you to go, wasn't it?'

'I . . . I happened to be in the district on another matter . . . '

'I see. It wouldn't be like *this* key, then?'

Hinton held up a key between his finger and thumb. Defoe stared at it.

'Where did you get that?' he muttered.

'We found it on the body of Madeleine Peters,' said Hinton.

Defoe shook his head.

'I've never seen it before,' he declared, and Hinton was convinced that he was lying.

'This opens the stage door of the Regency Theatre,' he said. 'Have you any idea how it came into the possession of Miss Peters?'

'No . . . I've no idea at all.'

'Don't you think it rather strange that she should have been in possession of a key to the Regency?'

'Yes . . . I — I can't account for it.'

'What did you do after she left you last night?' asked Hinton.

'I drove down to see some friends — near Sevenoaks.'

'What time did you arrive there?'

'Well, as a matter of fact, not until nearly midnight . . . '

'How was that?'

'I was unfortunate. My car broke down . . . '

'That was very unfortunate,' said Hinton. 'Were you alone all this time?'

'Yes — of course . . . '

'So from the time you left Miss Peters — say at eight o'clock — until you arrived at Sevenoaks at midnight, there is only your unsubstantiated word to say where you were?'

'Are you suggesting that I am lying, Inspector?' demanded Defoe.

'No, but we like to be able to check statements of this kind. What was wrong with your car?'

'I — I don't know. I'm not a very good mechanic. I got it to go eventually . . . more by luck than anything else.'

'I see.' Hinton's tone was a little dubious.

'I've told you the truth,' said Defoe, quickly.

'I'm not saying you haven't . . . '

'I know nothing about this — murder. I wasn't near the Regency Theatre last night.'

'No, but the point is you *could* have been. It's not very far to Sevenoaks. If you'd left after Miss Peters was killed, you would have had plenty of time to get there by midnight.'

'It's absurd,' said Defoe, but he looked white and troubled. 'Why should I want to kill her?'

'I'm not suggesting you did,' answered Hinton. 'But *somebody* did. It's my job to find out who that was . . . '

# 15

The company could talk about nothing else but the murder on the following morning. Whenever they were not actually rehearsing they would split up into little groups and discuss this latest development in the mystery of the Regency.

Maysie Sheringham tackled Tangye as soon as she had finished her second number.

'I say, Tangye,' she said, 'isn't it awful about Madeleine Peters?'

'Yes, I couldn't believe it when they told me.'

'I think I'd believe anything about this place.' Maysie looked round and shivered. 'It's beginning to give me the creeps.'

'They found her in the sealed dressing room . . .'

'I know. How on earth did she get in there?'

'That wasn't all they found . . .'

'You mean . . . Castleton Mayne?'

'Yes.'

'I think that was horrible,' said Maysie, 'almost more horrible than the murder . . . There must be some other way into that room.'

'The police couldn't find one.'

'All the same, there must be. It stands to reason . . . '

'There's not much use in talking about 'reason', Maysie. The whole thing's mad.'

'I really do believe you heard that knocking, now,' said Maysie.

'I told you I did . . . '

'I thought it was just imagination, darling. Of course there really was somebody in that room . . . '

'Who?'

'Why, the murderer, of course,' said Maysie. 'He knows the secret of how to get in and out of the place, and that's where he's been hiding.'

'Surely he'd hardly advertise that he was there by knocking?' said Tangye, reasonably.

'No,' answered Maysie. 'No, I suppose not . . . '

'There's somebody else who knows the secret, too,' went on Tangye. 'Mrs. Mayne. There were fresh flowers on the dressing table . . . '

''Ullo, you two — 'avin' a chinwag?' Nutty's voice broke in, cheerfully.

'Hello, Nutty,' said Tangye.

'I must go,' said Maysie, hurriedly. 'See you later, Tangye.'

She ran quickly away, and Nutty stared after her disconsolately.

'There yer are,' he said. 'Off like the wind. Blimey! Anyone'd think I was goin' ter eat 'er . . . '

Tangye laughed. At that moment Victor Price joined them.

'Well,' he said, 'what do you think of the latest, eh? Never a dull moment, is there?'

He looked round and lowered his voice.

'If this show ever opens it will be a miracle,' he said. 'Every time I come to rehearsal in the morning I wonder what's going to happen next.'

'Victor,' said Tangye suddenly, 'tell me something.'

'That depends on what it is,' he answered.

'How did you know what sort of dress I was wearing that night?' she asked. 'The night I was hit on the head . . . '

He grinned.

'That's easy,' he said. 'I saw you coming out of the Milan.'

So that was the explanation, she thought. So very simple. But was it the true one? Had he seen her come out of the Milan that night or had he . . . ? Clifford Brett called her and she was still wondering as she hurried to see what he wanted.

★　★　★

The police car pulled up outside the ugly house in Pimlico, and Inspector Hinton, accompanied by a Detective-Sergeant, got out and ascended the stone steps. He knocked.

'I shan't be sorry when we get this interview over,' he remarked, while they waited for an answer. 'It's likely to be unpleasant.'

228

The Sergeant, a man of few words, smiled sympathetically and said nothing. Mrs. Duppy opened the door.

'What . . . ? Oh, you're back again, are you?' she said, ungraciously. 'What d'you want this time?'

'I should like to see Mrs. Mayne,' said Hinton.

'Well, you can't,' she snapped. 'She's not well and she's in bed . . . '

'I'm afraid I must insist on seeing her,' said Hinton, firmly.

'Why can't you leave her alone?' demanded the old woman. 'She can't help you and you only upset her . . . '

'I'm afraid I shall have to see her, Mrs. Duppy. It's very important.'

'Oh, well, I s'pose you'd better come in . . . '

'Thank you. This is Detective-Sergeant Watkins.' Hinton introduced the silent man beside him.

'Two of you this time,' grumbled Mrs. Duppy as she shut the door. 'Aren't you ever going to give us any peace?'

'I don't enjoy coming here,' said Hinton, truthfully.

'I should've thought you did,' she retorted, leading the way up the stairs. 'Every time I open the door these days you're on the step. Mrs. Mayne's not very well. If you must see her I 'ope you'll make it as short as you can. I don't want her upset again.'

'I'm afraid what I have to say won't exactly please her,' said Hinton.

'Why, what is it?' The old woman gave him a sharp glance.

'There's no reason why you shouldn't be present during the interview. In fact I would prefer that you were.'

They stopped outside the door of Isobel Mayne's bedroom and Mrs. Duppy knocked softly.

'Are you awake, dearie?' she called.

A faint voice answered from within. 'Yes, what is it, Duppy?'

'Inspector Hinton's here again — with another man . . . '

'I won't see him,' called the voice. 'I don't want to see anyone. Send him away . . . '

'I'm sorry, Mrs. Mayne,' said Hinton, 'but . . . '

'Go away,' called Mrs. Mayne. 'I've nothing to say to you — nothing . . . '

'I must see you,' said Hinton.

'You'd better see them, dearie,' advised Mrs. Duppy.

'But I don't want to. Tell them to go away . . . '

'They won't go until they've seen you, dearie . . . '

'Am I never to get any peace or rest . . . Very well, very well . . . bring them in . . . '

Mrs. Duppy opened the door and they entered the bedroom. In a huge four-poster bed Mrs. Mayne lay, supported by several pillows. She looked older and thinner, but her voice was as resonant as ever. She regarded them with a cold, unfriendly stare.

'Well? What is it now? What is it?' she demanded impatiently.

'I think I should warn you to be prepared for a shock, Mrs. Mayne,' said Hinton, gently. 'Last night there was another murder at the Regency Theatre.'

Mrs. Duppy gave a little cry.

'Why come to me?' said Isobel Mayne.

'What do I know about it? I warned you — I warned all of you. The evil will go on. You cannot prevent it — none of you can prevent it.'

'Who was it?' breathed Duppy almost inaudibly.

'A woman named Madeleine Peters,' answered Hinton. 'I came to see you, Mrs. Mayne, because she was killed in the sealed room — your late husband's dressing room.'

Fear sprang into the faded eyes.

'It's not true,' said Isobel Mayne, huskily. 'It isn't true. Nobody could get in there. You're saying it to frighten me . . . The door is locked and sealed . . . I sealed it . . . '

'We had to break it open,' explained Hinton.

The woman in the bed uttered a strangled cry and sat forward.

'You — had — to — break — it — open?' she repeated.

Hinton nodded.

'Yes,' he said. 'We found the body of this woman, Peters, and . . . *you* know what else we found, Mrs. Mayne . . . '

'You broke open that room?' Her face was ashen and her month worked convulsively. 'What have you done?' she wailed. 'What have you done?'

'Now, dearie . . . ' began Mrs. Duppy, soothingly.

'Why didn't you tell us that your husband's body was there?' said Hinton.

'Tell you . . . *tell* you?' she said, scornfully. 'Why should I tell you? What had it to do with you or with anybody except me? Hadn't he a right to be there — in the place he loved? Wasn't it better than shutting him up in a tomb or burying him in the ground to rot away to dust and ugliness? I knew what he would have wished and I gave it to him. That dressing room was his coffin and the entire theatre his monument. Why couldn't he be left undisturbed?'

'*You* didn't leave him undisturbed, did you, Mrs. Mayne?' said Hinton.

'I was different,' she retorted. 'I was his wife. I had a right to visit my husband's tomb when I chose . . . '

'How did you get into that locked and sealed room?' asked Hinton. 'To put fresh flowers on the dressing table?'

Isobel Mayne turned towards Mrs. Duppy.

'Duppy,' she said, 'you've been talking . . .'

'No, dearie,' protested the old woman. 'No . . . I haven't said anything . . .'

'Then how do they know?' said Mrs. Mayne. 'How do they know, Duppy? Only you and I knew. Alexander didn't know — nobody knew . . .' She began to chuckle suddenly and her hands clawed at the covers. It was a horrible sound and even the phlegmatic Sergeant paled. 'For thirty years everybody believed that Castleton Mayne was buried . . . and all the time he was *there!*' She nodded several times. 'Yes . . . yes, there was nothing in the coffin they buried . . . only sand.' She laughed — a low, throaty chuckle. 'We took him out, didn't we, Duppy? We took him out and screwed it down again and they never noticed any difference . . .'

'Don't, dearie, don't,' whimpered Mrs. Duppy.

'It was right he should be there,' went

on Mrs. Mayne, 'just sitting at his dressing table — made up and ready to go on. I've seen him just like that — many, many times, waiting for his call . . . When I came in he would see me in the mirror and smile. Nobody guessed he was *still* there . . . no, no, they never guessed. They thought the old theatre was empty, didn't they? But we knew better, Duppy, didn't we?'

'Mrs. Mayne . . . ' began Hinton.

She looked at him without any sign of recognition.

'Who are you?' she demanded. 'What do you want here? I'll tell you nothing . . . ' She laughed. 'There's evil at the Regency . . . there's danger at the Regency . . . I warned them . . . I thought it would frighten them away. There *was* death there, wasn't there, Duppy? I only told them the truth . . . '

'Be quiet, dearie,' implored the old woman. 'Be quiet . . .

'Have you got the key, Duppy?' asked Mrs. Mayne, suddenly. 'Hide it . . . they mustn't know about *that* . . . not even Alexander. I shall want the key tonight

. . . It's time I took some fresh flowers . . . '

'Mrs. Mayne,' said Hinton earnestly, 'please try and understand me. Your husband is not there any longer.'

'Not there . . . not there? What do you mean? Who are these fools, Duppy? What are they talking about?'

'Now listen to me, dearie,' said Mrs. Duppy.

'Have they found out?' said Isobel Mayne. 'What have they done with him . . . ?'

'We had to remove your husband's body to the mortuary,' said Hinton.

'To the mortuary?' she cried. 'You mustn't take my husband *there* . . . ' She struggled up and raised a trembling hand. 'Listen, don't you understand? My husband isn't dead . . . not as long as you leave him in that dressing room. But if you take him away he'll die . . . he'll die . . . he'll die . . . ' She broke into a fit of hysterical sobbing.

Mrs. Duppy put an arm round her.

'Hush, dearie,' she said, 'don't go on like this . . . ' She looked at Hinton and shook her head. 'She's never been as bad as this before. It's your fault . . . coming here and worrying her . . . '

'I don't want to upset her too much,' said Hinton.

'The damage is done now,' said Mrs. Duppy. 'I wish you'd go. Maybe I could calm her down, then, and get her to sleep.'

Hinton decided that it was not much use remaining.

'All right,' he said, 'but we shall have to get a statement from both of you later . . . '

'Get rid of them, Duppy,' cried Mrs. Mayne. 'Get rid of them. I won't have them spying and poking about in my affairs . . . '

'Come along, Watkins,' said Hinton.

'Yes, yes, go!' screamed Isobel Mayne. 'And don't come here any more. I won't have you in my house . . . Duppy — they're not to be admitted, do you hear? They've killed my husband . . . they've killed . . . '

A spasm contorted her face and her words ended in a slurred groan. With her fingers clutching the air convulsively, she fell back on the pillows.

'What's the matter, dearie?' Mrs. Duppy, alarmed, bent over the bed. 'Oh, Lord o' mercy look at her face . . . '

'Send for a doctor, quickly . . . Here, you go, Watkins . . . ' Hinton leaned forward and looked at the old woman in the bed. 'I think she's had a stroke,' he said.

# 16

'I want to talk to you, Tangye,' said Keith Gilbert. 'You won't be wanted for a bit — Clifford's going through Maysie's numbers. Come outside in the passage.'

His voice was unusually serious and she looked at him in surprise.

'What's the matter?' she said.

He didn't answer until they were alone in the passage. Then he said:

'Did Clifford tell you what happened here last night?'

She nodded.

'Yes, it's horrible, isn't it? Madeleine Peters murdered and Castleton Mayne's body in that dressing-room all the time . . .'

'That was just an uncanny little idea of Mrs. Mayne's, I suppose,' he said. 'I can more or less understand *that*, although it's rather weird. It's all this other business that's worrying me.'

'Worrying you?' she said.

'Yes . . . you see, Tangye, until we know what it's all about we don't know what may happen next. There have already been two murders.'

'You mean . . . you think there may be — more?'

'I don't know . . . that's what's so frightening,' he answered, seriously. 'There's a pattern somewhere and the murderer's working it out piece by piece . . . Alexander Mayne was part of it, and so was Madeleine Peters. Others may become part of it, unconsciously perhaps, because they don't know what the pattern is . . . It might be you . . . or me . . . '

Tangye's eyes widened.

'Keith — you're frightening me . . . '

'I don't want to frighten you, darling,' he said, 'but I want you to be on your guard. Until this thing is cleared up, and we *know* what's behind it all, I want you to promise me that you'll never come here alone or stay here alone . . . not even for a moment . . . '

'I'll willingly promise that,' she declared. 'I'm scared to death of the place.'

'I don't say there is any danger for

*you*,' said Keith, 'but there might be . . . if you heard, or saw, something that was likely to upset this unknown person's plan . . . '

'Do you think that's why Madeleine Peters was killed?' she asked.

'Yes, I do. I think she stumbled on something that was dangerous . . . to someone . . . '

'Keith,' she said, suddenly. 'Do you know what I think? I think there's something hidden in this theatre that somebody's looking for . . . '

'But what could it be?' he asked.

'I don't know . . . but it would account for all the things that have happened, wouldn't it?'

'Yes.' He rubbed his chin thoughtfully. 'If somebody has been searching for something, it must have been a nasty shock when the theatre was re-opened . . . '

'While the theatre was closed they had the run of it, you see?' she said. 'It all fits . . . '

'Alexander Mayne surprised this person when he came that morning to

241

show us over the place ... I think you've got something, Tangye ... '

Hurried footsteps interrupted them. Olivia Winter came quickly up to them.

'Good morning,' she said, briskly. 'Is Mr. Macdonald here?'

'I haven't seen him,' said Keith.

'He said he would be here,' she said with a frown. 'He asked me to bring these contracts, if they arrived.'

'Perhaps he's somewhere in the front of the house?' he suggested.

'I'll see if I can find him.' She was turning away when she thought of something and came back. 'Is it true that Madeleine Peters was murdered here last night?' she asked.

'Yes, in Castleton Mayne's old dressing room,' said Keith.

'The sealed room? But how could anyone get in there?'

'That's another puzzle to add to the rest, Miss Winter,' he said. 'The seals were intact. Inspector Hinton had to break open the door.'

'They've screened it round,' said Tangye. 'Look ... ' She nodded in the direction of the dressing room. A screen of wood and canvas had been fastened over the shattered door. Olivia Winter deliberately turned her head away.

'I don't want to look,' she said. 'This place — frightens me. I know you think I'm silly, but I don't believe there's a practical explanation for these murders and — and the other things. There's something in this theatre that isn't human . . . that wants to be left alone . . . '

'I'm surprised that a woman like you should believe in such things,' said Keith.

'I have made a study of the occult, and I am convinced that such things *do* exist,' she retorted.

'Ghosts, do you mean?' asked Tangye.

'Earthbound spirits,' answered Olivia, 'and other more dreadful things. Cleverer people than I have believed in them . . . '

'You really believe that this theatre is haunted?' said Keith.

'Yes, Mr. Gilbert,' she answered. 'By something malignant and dangerous.'

'Well, it's not Castleton Mayne,' he said. 'They found his body, preserved by some form of embalming, in that room last night when they broke in . . . '

She looked at him in horrified amazement.

'*Preserved?*' she whispered. 'Castleton Mayne? In there?'

'Yes.'

'But don't you see?' she went on quickly. 'Don't you understand? That accounts for everything . . . '

Keith shook his head in bewilderment.

'Castleton Mayne should have been buried thirty years ago,' she continued rapidly. 'The natural processes of dissolution have been tampered with, and the repercussion on the psychic plane has had a dreadful result. The spirit has remained chained to the body which should have long since disintegrated. Castleton Mayne has become one of the *undead.*'

'Oh, don't,' breathed Tangye, 'don't . . . '

'I'm surprised at ye, Miss Winter,' interrupted the voice of Macdonald, scathingly. 'I never heard such a lot of balderdash in my life.'

He had come upon them without their hearing his approach.

'It's nothing of the kind, Mr. Macdonald,' she said. 'If you had made a study of the subject you would realize that.'

'Do ye honestly believe in all that nonsense?' asked Macdonald curiously.

'Yes, I do,' she answered, defiantly.

He shook his head.

'And I always thought ye were a clever, practical woman,' he said.

'It is possible to be both,' she replied. Abruptly she changed the subject: 'Here are the contracts you asked for. If there's nothing more you want me to do, I'll go back to the office.'

He took the envelope she gave him and tucked it under his arm.

'I'll look through these an' sign them,' he said. 'Ye might ring up Cowan and tell him that ye'll be bringing them round this afternoon.'

'Very well.' She said goodbye and hurried efficiently away.

'Were you listening to all that?' asked Keith.

Macdonald nodded.

'I came through from the stage,' he

began, and stopped as there came from the direction of the stage door a high, shrill scream.

'Oh, God! What was that?' cried Tangye.

'Miss Winter . . . ' Macdonald went racing down the passage, his long legs covering the ground at an amazing speed. They followed as fast as they could. Olivia Winter, her face white as chalk, was leaning against the wall by the stage door.

'Why did ye scream? What's the matter?' demanded Macdonald.

She pointed to the stage doorkeeper's box.

'Look,' she stammered, 'look . . . in there . . . '

They looked in the small cubbyhole. The old man, Savernick, was slumped forward in his chair and there was blood everywhere . . .

'Look . . . at his throat,' whispered Keith in a voice that was hoarse and unnatural. 'Look at his . . . throat . . . '

'He was killed while he was telephoning,' said Macdonald. 'The receiver's still in his hand . . . '

The silence that followed was broken by Macdonald. He said, staring at the thing in the chair:

'He was killed in the same way as Alexander Mayne . . . '

'And Madeleine Peters,' said Keith.

'When is this going to stop?' whispered Tangye. 'It's dreadful.'

'Ye found Savernick like this when ye were going out, Miss Winter?' Macdonald turned to the secretary. She nodded weakly.

'Yes . . . I was just going to say goodbye . . . and then I saw all the . . . blood . . . '

'He was all right when you came in?' asked Keith.

'Yes . . . he spoke to me . . . '

'Then it must have happened while you were talking to us.'

'Who could have done it?' said Tangye.

'The stage door's open . . . anybody could have slipped in,' replied Macdonald.

'Why should anyone want to kill that old man?' said the girl.

'I don't know . . . there was a bit of a

mystery about him, wasn't there . . . Here's Nutty.'

''Ullo,' said the little man cheerily, and then as he saw: 'Blimey, what's 'appened?'

'Savernick's been murdered,' said Keith.

Nutty pursed up his lips to whistle, thought better of it, and stopped.

'Lumme,' he said, 'somebody's fond o' stickin' knives in people's throats round 'ere, ain't they? This makes the third . . . '

'We've got to find out who's responsible,' declared Keith. 'Nobody's safe until we do . . . '

'He was killed while he was talking to somebody on the telephone,' said Tangye. 'He's still holding the receiver. Do you think the line's still connected?'

'Ye mean the person at the other end may have heard something?' said Macdonald, quickly.

'It's a chance, isn't it?' asked Tangye.

'We can't touch anything until the police have seen him,' said Keith. 'We'd better tell Clifford. Would you go, Miss Winter?'

'Yes, of course . . . '

'Don't let anyone else hear what ye say,' said Macdonald.

She nodded and hurried away.

'If yer ask me,' said Nutty, 'there's somebody barmy at the back of all this . . . A ravin', blinkin' maniac with all the bats in the world loose in 'is belfry. There ain't no ruddy sense to it.'

They didn't answer. The theory was not only plausible, it seemed the most likely. In a short while Brett, looking worried and anxious, joined them.

'This is terrible,' he said. 'It's got to be stopped. There's a wholesale killer loose and probably as mad as a hatter.'

'That's what Nutty thinks,' said Keith.

'That's what I'm beginning to think, too,' said Brett. 'We must notify the police . . . '

'About what?' asked the quiet voice of Inspector Hinton.

They looked round. He was standing in the open stage door.

'You couldn't have turned up at a more opportune moment,' said Brett. 'Look at this . . . '

Hinton looked.

'Savernick,' he murmured. 'When did this happen?'

'Only a few minutes ago . . . '

'Who discovered it?'

'I did,' said Olivia. She explained the circumstances briefly.

'Somebody must have come in the stage door, killed him, and slipped away again,' said Macdonald. 'It would have been quite easy . . . '

'Yes . . . I see,' said Hinton. 'Quite easy . . . '

'He was telephoning when he was killed,' said Keith. 'We wondered if they heard anything at the other end . . . '

'They didn't,' answered Hinton, to his surprise. 'Nothing of importance.'

'How do you know that?' demanded Keith.

'He was telephoning to Scotland Yard. That's why I got here so opportunely . . . '

'To Scotland Yard . . . *Savernick?*' said Brett.

'Yes . . . you see, I arranged for him to apply for this job,' said Hinton, calmly. 'I didn't think he'd have much trouble in getting it.'

'*You* arranged . . . I don't understand . . . '

'I wanted someone to keep an eye on things for me,' explained Hinton, 'and report anything he found out. I sent Detective-Sergeant James Savernick.'

# 17

There was great activity in the Regency Theatre. The stage was a confusion of noise and men, hammering, shouting, and struggling with heavy pieces of scenery as they prepared for the dress rehearsal. Victor Price was here there and everywhere as he tried to bring some semblance of order out of chaos.

'Up on yer long . . . No, no . . . too much . . . Drop her a little . . . Now up on yer short . . . That's better . . . centre a fraction . . . That's it. Tie off . . . Right . . . take her up . . . '

The huge painted backcloth, like a great coloured sail, went swishing up into the shadows of the grid . . .

'Hi Bill . . . drop that set o' lines, will yer? Be'ind number four border . . . '

Price called to a man on the 'catwalk'.

'Electrics!'

'Yes?'

'Have you got those ambers in the

252

spots in number one batten?'

'Doin' it next,' shouted the electrician above the surrounding din. 'We're just doin' the blues . . . '

'O.K. Have you done the front floods?'
'Yes.'

Clifford Brett came quickly down to the stage manager.

'How's it going, Victor?' he asked.

'Not too bad, Mr. Brett,' answered Price. 'We're a bit behind. They were late sending some of the stuff . . . '

'Will you be ready in time for the dress rehearsal?'

'I think so . . . we're doing our best . . . ' He broke off suddenly. 'Hi! That cloth's got to be battened out . . . Excuse me, Mr. Brett . . . '

He hurried away upstage to a group of men who were bending over a spread-out sheet of canvas.

'Will they be ready, Clifford?'

Brett turned to find Ronnie Hays at his side.

'I doubt it,' he replied with a shrug. 'Have you ever known a dress rehearsal start on time?'

There was a shout from the prompt side.

'Try them tabs now, Jack . . . '

With a swish the ivory satin tabs closed smoothly on their runners.

'O.K.,' called the voice, 'take 'em back . . . '

'I hope we get through without any trouble,' said Hays.

'I don't see why not,' said Brett, watching the tabs open. 'It's been running pretty smoothly at rehearsals . . . '

'I don't mean *that* kind of trouble,' said Hays.

'Oh, I see.' Brett nodded. 'Well, there hasn't been anything since Savernick was killed, and that's over a week ago. Perhaps there won't be any more . . . '

'I wonder what the police are doing? You haven't heard anything, have you?'

'Not a thing,' said Brett. 'The last time I saw Hinton was when he brought that expert to examine the door of Castleton Mayne's dressing room. I think they found something, but they didn't tell me . . . '

'How the trick was worked, do you mean?'

'Yes.'

'It seems queer,' said Ronnie. 'All sorts of things happen . . . including three murders . . . and then . . . nothing . . . '

'Let's be thankful it has stopped,' grunted Brett.

'*If* it has,' said Hays, doubtfully.

Maysie Sheringham came running up to them, worried and anxious.

'Mr. Brett,' she said, 'they haven't sent my dress for the flower number. What shall I do?'

'I'll get on to them, Maysie,' he answered. 'Everything else all right?'

'Yes.'

''Ullo, Miss Sheringham,' greeted Nutty, appearing from behind a pile of scenery. 'Look 'ere, wot about . . . '

'Excuse me,' she said hurriedly, without giving him time to complete the sentence, 'I've got so much to do . . . '

She was gone before he could say another word. He looked after her disgustedly.

'Blimey,' he said, 'you'd think I was a blinkin' wild animal the way she 'ops off when I speaks to 'er . . . '

Ronnie laughed.

'A wolf, Nutty . . . that's what you are,' he said.

'Ronnie!' Keith Gilbert called from the back of the stage. 'Have you seen Tangye anywhere?'

'Isn't she in her dressing room?'

'No . . . Victor, have *you* seen Miss Ward?'

'No, Mr. Gilbert, I don't think she's come in yet . . . You'll have to change that border over, Jeff. It's got to come in front of the cloth.'

Gilbert came down and joined Nutty and Ronnie Hays.

'She's leaving it rather late, isn't she?' he said.

'We shan't be ready for hours yet,' said Hays.

'I know, but she's got her dresses to . . . '

''Ere she is now,' interrupted Nutty.

Keith went to meet her as she picked her way quickly across the littered stage.

'Hello, darling,' he said, 'I was just wondering what had happened to you . . . '

'Why?' she said. 'I've heaps of time. I suddenly remembered I wanted some number five and a blue liner . . . '

Brett came running towards them.

'Nutty,' he cried breathlessly, 'be a good fellow and go along to Layton's for me, will you? They've sent the wrong wigs . . . Grab a taxi.'

'Okey doke,' said Nutty, obligingly.

'I've been on the phone to them,' called Brett after him. 'They know you're coming . . . '

'Right . . . be back in a jiffy!' shouted Nutty, and disappeared through the iron door at the back of the stage.

'I must go,' said Tangye. 'See you later, Keith . . . '

'All right, darling,' he said, and when she had gone, 'What about a drink, you chaps? They won't be ready here for ages . . . '

'It'll have to be a quick one,' said Clifford Brett. 'I mustn't be long . . . '

They left the babel and the confusion of the stage, congratulating themselves that the mysterious happenings at the Regency seemed to have come to a stop. In this they were a little premature . . .

★ ★ ★

The door into the darkened room was opened softly and Mrs. Duppy peered in. There was no sound, and after a moment she called gently:

'Are you awake, dearie?'

'Yes, Duppy,' answered Mrs. Mayne, weakly.

The old woman came into the room, switched on a shaded lamp, and approached the bed.

'I've brought you some warm milk,' she said.

Isobel Mayne turned her head on the pillow slightly.

'I . . . I don't think . . . I want anything,' she said.

'Now just try and drink it, dearie,' said Mrs. Duppy, persuasively. She slipped an arm beneath the frail shoulders and raised her up. 'There now . . . come along . . . '

Isobel Mayne sipped at the milk that was held to her lips.

'You . . . you're very good to me, Duppy,' she murmured.

'Don't be silly, dearie, I'm nothing of the kind . . . '

'Yes, you are . . . you've always been good to me . . . '

'Well, I'm very fond of you, dearie . . . ' There were tears in Mrs. Duppy's eyes.

'I know . . . I . . . I can't drink any more . . . '

'Very well.' Mrs. Duppy set the glass down on the bedside table. 'Now I'll just smooth your pillows and then you can go to sleep . . . '

'I . . . don't want to go to sleep, Duppy . . . '

'You know what the doctor said,' answered Mrs. Duppy. 'You must rest as much as possible . . . '

Isobel Mayne uttered a short, fluttering sigh. 'I shall soon,' she said. 'Such a long rest, Duppy . . . Stay and talk to me . . . '

'All right, dearie. What shall we talk about . . . ?'

The deep-set eyes in the wrinkled face on the pillow looked at her. They were dim. The fire that once had sparkled there was almost burned out.

'I've been thinking,' said Isobel Mayne.

'Do you . . . do you remember . . . the first time . . . I played Juliet?'

'Of course I do,' said Mrs. Duppy. 'You looked beautiful, dearie.'

'I was . . . so nervous . . . waiting for my cue . . . '

'Everybody said you gave a wonderful performance, dearie. Your dressing room was so full of flowers we could scarcely move, could we?'

The dim eyes were growing dimmer. The feeble mind had gone back through the years to that moment of triumph . . .

'I . . . I couldn't remember . . . a line . . . waiting there . . . in the wings.'

'You were all right when you went on, dearie . . . '

'Yes . . . it all came back to me then . . . I've been trying to remember Juliet's entrance . . . Can you . . . remember, Duppy?'

'How now, who calls?' said Mrs. Duppy.

'That's it . . . '*How now, who calls?*' Fancy you remembering, Duppy . . . '

'I watched you from the side so often,' said the old woman. 'Lovely, you looked.

260

You oughtn't to talk too much, you'll tire yourself . . . '

'No . . . no, Duppy, I won't . . . I want to talk . . . There's nobody . . . to talk to now . . . only you, Duppy . . . '

'I'll always be here, dearie . . . '

There was a short silence. The room was very still. High up in the old carved cornice the shadows were thick. They seemed to be getting thicker. There were shadows, too, in the eyes of the woman in the bed. Were they, also, thickening . . . ?

'Duppy?' The faint voice broke the silence. 'Where is . . . Alexander?'

'Don't you remember, dearie?'

'Oh, yes . . . how stupid of me . . . I'd forgotten . . . I warned him, didn't I? I warned him . . . '

'Now, don't start worrying yourself again, dearie,' said Mrs. Duppy, soothingly.

'Did you . . . order . . . the flowers?' went on the weak voice. 'It's time we took some fresh flowers, Duppy . . . '

Mrs. Duppy sighed. It would be better not to argue.

'I'll see to it, dearie,' she said.

'I scared them, Duppy.' Isobel Mayne gave a feeble chuckle. 'I scared them . . . one morning. I was in there . . . and I knocked . . . on the inside of the door . . . You should . . . have heard . . . that girl scream . . . They never found out . . . the secret, did they?' For an instant her mind cleared and she remembered: '*Oh*, they *did* . . . they did find out . . . '

She tried to sit up in her agitation.

'Yes, yes, they found out,' said Mrs. Duppy, gently pushing her back on the pillow.

'They took . . . him away . . . they took him away . . . Where did they take him, Duppy? We must . . . get him back . . . '

'There, there. You're upsetting yourself. Try and go to sleep now, dearie . . . '

'How can I sleep? There isn't time . . . '

'What do you mean, dearie?' asked Mrs. Duppy.

'We shall be late . . . '

'For what, dearie, for what?' said the old woman, gently stroking the thin hand that plucked at the coverlet.

'For the . . . theatre,' said Isobel

Mayne, impatiently. 'Don't you remember? I'm playing Juliet . . . '

Mrs. Duppy shook her head sadly. The tears gathered in her eyes.

'Oh, dearie . . . ' she said, helplessly.

'Get my dress,' whispered Isobel Mayne. 'It's a lovely dress . . . isn't it, Duppy?'

'Yes, dearie, yes . . . It's a lovely dress . . . '

The woman in the bed sat up, and Mrs. Duppy supported her on her arm.

'The house . . . is packed . . . Do you . . . think they'll like me . . . ?'

'Dearie . . . '

'I'm so . . . nervous . . . Duppy, do hurry . . . Get me . . . into my dress . . . '

In the street outside a barrel organ suddenly began to play.

Mrs. Mayne turned her head.

'Listen . . . listen, Duppy,' she breathed, excitedly. 'There's the overture . . . I'm not even made up yet . . . I'll never be ready . . . '

'You'll be all right, dearie,' said Mrs. Duppy, the tears running down her withered cheeks.

'It's getting near . . . my cue,' whispered Mrs. Mayne, clutching her hand tightly. 'What do I . . . say, Duppy? I can't remember . . . What do I say?'

'"How now, who calls?"'

'Yes, yes . . . I don't know what I . . . should do . . . without you, Duppy . . . '

'Dearie . . . Oh, dearie . . . '

'It's nearly time . . . for my entrance . . . Don't talk to me . . . more . . . '

No sound in that shadowy room, not even the sound of a breath. Only the barrel organ in the street, grinding out its endless tune.

'Wish me luck, Duppy . . . wish me luck . . . ' The voice was barely audible.

'Yes, dearie, yes . . . '

There was faint sobbing now mingled with the tune from the barrel organ. And then, suddenly, a loud, sweet, resonant voice sounded through the room:

'*How now, who calls?*'

Isobel Mayne made her entrance . . . and her exit . . .

# 18

Out of the chaos which had reigned over the stage of the Regency Theatre had come something like order. The first scene of the revue was set, and the cast stood about in little groups, talking and laughing, and waiting for the arrival of Clifford Brett to inspect their dresses. He came hurrying in with Keith Gilbert, Ronnie Hays, and Nutty, just as Tangye appeared on the stage in her first scene dress.

'Will I do?' she asked.

'Yes, you look very nice,' he said, eyeing her critically. 'All your other dresses fit you?'

'Yes.'

'Good — I'd better see the rest of 'em . . . Victor!'

'Yes, Mr. Brett?' The perspiring stage manager appeared from behind a canvas flat.

'Get everybody on the stage for a dress

parade,' said Brett. 'I'm going down into the stalls.'

He made his way through the pass-door. In the stalls he met Macdonald. The agent was hot and looked worried.

'Hello, Brett,' he greeted. 'Ye've no started yet?'

'No, just going to,' said Brett.

'I hurried here from the office as fast as I could,' said Macdonald. 'A rather queer thing has happened . . . '

'Oh, no — not any more,' said Brett.

'I was working late when the telephone bell rang,' explained Macdonald, hurriedly. 'Miss Winter had gone home to change for the rehearsal so I took the call myself . . . '

'Well, go on . . . ' said Brett, as he paused.

'Wait while I get my breath . . . It was a queer sort of voice that spoke — a kind of whisper. It said: 'Tell Clifford Brett he'll never finish the dress rehearsal . . . ' '

'It didn't say what was going to stop me?' said Brett.

Macdonald shook his head.

266

'No, whoever it was rang off . . . '

Brett looked thoughtful for a moment. Then he turned to Keith and Hays.

'Look, you chaps,' he said. 'Make a thorough search of the theatre, will you? We'll make sure there's nobody here who shouldn't be. Mac — will you go with them? I can't come — I must O.K. these dresses.'

'Leave it to us, Clifford,' said Keith.

'We'd better split up,' said Hays. 'I'll take the gallery . . . '

They made a thorough search of the entire theatre. And they found — nothing.

\* \* \*

Detective-Sergeant Boler came quickly along the stone corridor, stopped at the closed door of Inspector Hinton's office, and tapped.

Hinton's voice, muffled by the closed door, invited him to come in. He entered, shutting the door behind him.

'Well?' said Hinton, looking up from his desk. 'Did you get anything?'

'Yes, sir. I've got quite a lot — all you want, I think.'

'Sit down,' said Hinton. 'Pull up that chair . . . '

Boler sat down.

'Now,' continued the Inspector, 'let's have it . . . '

Boler produced a fat and battered notebook. He frowned at it for a moment and then looked up.

'I concentrated first on the — er — the person you mentioned, sir,' he began. 'It took me a long time to trace the history, but I've got it all here. You were right, sir . . . '

Hinton nodded gravely.

'I thought I might be,' he said, quietly. 'Go on . . . '

'Do you remember Harry Veeler?' asked Boler.

Hinton pursed his lips, and his forehead wrinkled.

'Harry Veeler,' he repeated, 'Harry Veeler? 'Con man'?'

'No, sir . . . burglar . . . '

Hinton's face cleared.

'I remember him . . . Harry the Cat

. . . That's the fellow, isn't it?'

'That's the feller, sir . . . '

'But he's dead, isn't he?' said Hinton. 'If I remember, he escaped from prison eighteen months ago and was found dead at the side of a country road. He was terribly injured and it was concluded that he'd been knocked down by a motor vehicle of some sort while trying to make his getaway . . . '

'That's quite right, sir,' said Boler.

'Then how the deuce does he come into this?' demanded Hinton.

'Do you recollect what he was sentenced for, sir?'

'Burglary, I suppose . . . That was his line . . . '

'Yes, sir . . . The Duchess of Easthanger's emeralds . . . '

Hinton sat up.

'By Jupiter! *That* was Veeler, was it?'

'Yes, sir. He tore a glove while he was climbing a pipe to the bedroom window and left his thumb-print behind. It was a piece of bad luck — for him. He'd never have been convicted otherwise, but the evidence of the print was conclusive. The emeralds — worth about eighty thousand pounds — were never found. He refused to say what he had done with 'em . . . '

'I still can't see the connection . . . '

'Veeler was call boy at the Regency Theatre when Castleton Mayne had it, sir . . . '

'Ah! Now we're getting warmer,' exclaimed Hinton. 'Go on, Sergeant.'

'We're going to get very hot in a second, sir,' said Boler. 'Harry Veeler was also the brother of . . . the person whose name you marked in red on that list . . . '

'Are you *sure?*'

'Quite sure, sir. I've got all the facts here.' Boler tapped his notebook.

Hinton leaned forward on the desk.

'Now we *are* getting somewhere,' he said with satisfaction. 'Wait a minute . . . let me think . . . The Duchess of Easthanger's emeralds were never found . . . Veeler was, in his youth, call boy at the Regency Theatre . . . At the time of the robbery the Regency had been shut for years and there was no likelihood of its being re-opened . . . Veeler wanted somewhere to hide those emeralds . . .

what better place could he have found than the old theatre where he had worked as a boy ... Boler,' Hinton brought his fist down with a crash on the desk, 'the Easthanger emeralds are hidden somewhere in the Regency Theatre. That's the motive behind all this.'

'That's how I worked it out, sir,' agreed the Sergeant.

'Of course. Now that we know Harry Veeler was once call boy there, and that he was related to — the person on that list, it sticks out a mile. It accounts for what's been happening, too. Ever since Veeler died this person has been looking for those emeralds ... '

'Yes, sir,' said Boler.

'But why did they have to search for them?' muttered Hinton, frowning. 'Why, if Veeler had told them where they were hidden, couldn't they have got them at the first attempt?'

'I think I can suggest an answer to that, sir,' said Boler. 'Veeler escaped from prison with the assistance of someone outside ... '

'You mean this person we're talking about?'

'Yes.' Boler nodded. 'This is what I believe happened, sir. While they're getting away, Veeler is knocked down and injured by this car or whatever it was. But he doesn't die at once. He lives long enough to say that the emeralds are hidden in the Regency, but not exactly where.'

'That's it,' said Hinton. 'I believe you've got it, Boler. From then on our friend has been searching for them. They were in the theatre when Mayne opened it that morning — that's why he was killed. And they were there again the night that Gilbert saw the torch . . . It all fits very nicely. Everything was done to scare people away, and they must have discovered the secret of that dressing room, too . . . '

'What was the secret of that, sir?' asked Boler.

'It was quite simple. The door was set in a wooden frame, like all other doors, but in this case the frame itself was the door. The entire frame opened on hinges.

The door *in* the frame could be locked and sealed, but it didn't make any difference — the whole thing opened when you knew the trick. Mrs. Mayne must have had it done so that she could pay periodical visits to her husband . . . '

'That was a weird idea,' remarked Boler, 'having him sort of preserved . . . '

'Horrible — but understandable when you realize her mental state. She's crazy as a coot. She thought the theatre was the most fitting tomb. There's a lot in it — if you look at it from her point of view . . . '

'What was this woman, Madeleine Peters, doing in the place?'

'I don't know, but she was killed for the same reason as Alexander Mayne. She surprised the murderer searching. She was probably hit on the head, dragged into that dressing room, and killed there, with the idea that her body wouldn't be found. It wouldn't if the blood hadn't oozed under the door . . . '

'The murderer don't stick at much, sir,' said Boler.

'There's eighty thousand pounds worth of emeralds at stake, don't forget,' said

Hinton. 'I should imagine there's a queer streak, too. We'll have to go pretty warily . . . '

'Aren't you going to make an arrest?'

'No, no,' answered Hinton, quickly. 'We've no real evidence. The fact that we can prove a relationship with Harry Veeler wouldn't convince a jury. Savernick discovered something, I think, but unfortunately the killer got in first . . . '

'What are you going to do, then, sir?' asked the Sergeant.

'We've got to catch this person in the act,' replied Hinton. 'That's the only thing that'll do us any good. I've got a vague idea which might work, but we've got to handle it very carefully . . . and it may be dangerous . . . very dangerous . . . '

★　★　★

Phillip Defoe came out of the Milan and called to the porter.

'Get me a taxi, George,' he said.

'Yes, sir.' The man went out into the road, and Defoe lighted a cigarette and

274

waited impatiently. He was unusually lucky for an empty taxi came almost immediately.

'Here you are, sir,' said George, riding up on the running-board. 'Where shall I tell 'im ter go, sir?'

'Tell him to drop me near Oxford Circus,' said Defoe. He got into the cab, dropped a coin into George's willing hand, and was driven off . . .

★　★　★

The dress rehearsal was in full swing. Sitting in the stalls, Clifford Brett watched scene after scene and decided it was a good show. There had been few hitches, and these were nothing serious. They were nearing the end of the first half and nothing had happened to justify the warning Macdonald had received over the telephone. Perhaps nothing would. It might quite easily have been only a try-on to scare them . . .

The tabs closed on Maysie Sheringham's number, the lights went down, and the front spots concentrated a circle of amber for Tangye's entrance. The orchestra began to play the introduction to her song, the tabs parted slowly to reveal her, dressed in a huge crinoline gown, standing on a rostrum. She began to walk slowly down a short flight of steps . . .

And then it happened.

Two shots in quick succession echoed through the theatre. Tangye screamed, swayed, and crumpled up in a heap in the middle of the stage . . .

# 19

Keith was the first to reach Tangye's side.

'Are you hurt?' he asked, huskily. 'Are you hurt?'

She looked up at him a little dazedly.

'No . . . no, I don't think so,' she said. 'It grazed my arm . . . '

He saw the blood on her dress and his face was white. But the wound in her arm was slight. The bullet had furrowed the flesh and it was bleeding freely, but it was only skin deep.

'Those shots came from the circle,' shouted Brett.

'Who's up there . . . ?'

There was the sound of a struggle at the back of the stalls, and Nutty's voice called breathlessly:

'I've got the blighter . . . 'Ere — give me a 'and someone . . . '

'I'm coming,' answered Macdonald, and went racing up the gangway. Brett followed him.

'Hold him, Nutty,' he cried, 'we're coming . . . '

Macdonald was the first to reach the struggling pair and he caught Nutty's captive by the arm.

'All right,' he said, 'I've got him . . . Stop struggling, will ye?'

But the man only redoubled his efforts. He fought and kicked like a maniac and it was not until Brett joined in the fray that he was overcome.

'Who is it?' panted Brett. 'Bring him out here into the light . . . '

They dragged the struggling man down the gangway, and as the light fell on his flushed face Brett uttered an exclamation.

'Defoe!'

Phillip Defoe glared at him.

'Let me go . . . ' he gasped, trying to shake himself free.

'Not ruddy likely!' said Nutty. 'What, after yer tried to kill Tangye? Take us fer blinkin' loonies?'

'I did not try to kill her . . . ' snapped Defoe.

'You shot at her, anyway,' said Brett, grimly.

'I did not . . .'

'Cor lumme, that's a good one,' broke in Nutty. 'I caught yer sneaking down the stairs from the circle . . .'

'I tell you I did not fire those shots,' declared Defoe. He was white and frightened. He looked from one to the other of them, little nervous glances, and moistened his dry lips with the tip of his tongue.

'Who did, then?' demanded Brett. 'If you were up in the circle you must have seen who it was . . .'

'I saw the flashes in the dark, but that was all . . .'

'See if he has a gun on him, one of ye,' said Macdonald.

'I haven't,' snarled Defoe, 'I keep telling you I had nothing to do with it . . .'

'I expect he chucked it away when 'e found we was on to 'im,' said Nutty.

They searched him, but there was no gun.

'He hasn't got it on him,' said Brett.

'I never had it,' declared Defoe. 'It wasn't me . . .'

'I'll go and look in the circle,' put in Hays. 'He probably threw it down there . . . '

'I keep telling you,' began Defoe.

'You shut up!' said Nutty. 'We don't want to hear any more of yer lies.'

Defoe started to speak and then stopped and shrugged his shoulders.

'Victor,' shouted Brett. 'Put the house lights on, will you?'

'O.K.,' called the stage manager.

There was a second's delay and then the lights all over the theatre blazed to life.

'Look here,' said Macdonald, 'if you didn't fire those shots, what were ye doin' in the theatre at all?'

'I came to see Brett,' muttered Defoe.

'I wasn't in the circle,' said Brett.

'No, but . . . '

The arrival of Keith interrupted him.

'Tangye's all right,' he said. 'Only a graze on her arm, but it was a near thing . . . ' He glared at Defoe. 'You did it, did you?'

'No, I didn't do it,' retorted Defoe. 'Why should I want to harm Miss Ward?'

'I don't know,' snapped Keith. 'Perhaps you'll tell the police.'

'The police . . . ?' Defoe looked even more frightened.

'Yes, I've telephoned Scotland Yard,' said Keith, curtly.

'You . . . you can't have me arrested,' expostulated Defoe. 'I haven't done anything. I came here to see Brett. He was busy with the rehearsal and . . . and I went up into the circle to watch . . . That's all . . . there's nothing criminal in that . . . '

'There's no sign of a pistol up here,' called Hays from the circle.

'Come on,' said Nutty. 'Stop lyin'. What did yer do with it?'

'I never had it,' said Defoe. 'I don't know anything about this shooting . . . You've got to believe me!'

'Believe yer?' cried Nutty. 'Cor lumme, I'd just as soon believe a viper wasn't poisonous . . . '

'Mr. Brett.' Olivia Winter appeared quietly and efficiently from somewhere.

'What is it, Miss Winter?' asked Brett.

'Is this what you're looking for?' She

held out her hand. In it lay a small automatic pistol.

'That's it!' exclaimed Nutty.

'Where did you find it?' demanded Macdonald.

'Just down there.' She nodded towards the back of the stalls. 'It was behind that last row of seats.'

Brett looked at Defoe.

'So that's where you dropped it, eh?' he said.

'No, no.' Defoe shook his head violently. 'I did not . . . I did not . . . '

'Excuse me, Mr. Brett,' said Olivia. 'It wasn't Mr. Defoe.'

'What?'

'I saw who dropped that pistol,' she went on quietly. 'It was Mr. Potts . . . '

★ ★ ★

Detective-Inspector Hinton sat in one of the dressing rooms. Sergeant Boler stood beside him, stolid, his face completely without expression. The others were clustered about the door. Defoe, reduced to a sullen fury, stood silently staring at the floor. Only the twitching of a small muscle at one corner of his mouth showed his nervousness.

Hinton looked up from the notes he had been taking.

'Now, Mr. Defoe,' he said, 'let me get this right. You say you came here to see Mr. Brett?'

Defoe nodded.

'Yes, but he was busy and so . . . '

'Just a minute, please,' interrupted Hinton, holding up his hand, 'we'll come to that later. You entered the theatre by the stage door, but there was nobody about, so you made your way to the auditorium through the pass-door. Mr. Brett was busy with the dress rehearsal, so you went up into the circle. Is that right?'

'Quite right,' agreed Defoe. 'I had only been there a few seconds . . . '

'When two shots were fired?' said Hinton.

'Yes, I saw the flashes in the dark and heard Miss Ward scream . . . '

'And then you heard somebody leave the circle hurriedly by the exit door?'

'Yes.'

'You didn't see who it was?'

'No, the shots were unexpected . . . I was startled. When I recovered from my surprise I ran out of the circle and down the stairs . . . '

'Where you encountered Mr. Potts?'

'Yes.'

'He was coming up from below?'

''Course I was comin' up,' broke in Nutty, belligerently. 'What d'yer think yer tryin' ter make out, eh?'

'I'm trying to get the whole thing clear, Mr. Potts,' said the Inspector, quietly. 'You struggled with Mr. Defoe and dragged him into the stalls?'

'That's right.'

Hinton turned to Olivia Winter.

'And it was then, you say, that you saw Mr. Potts throw away this automatic, Miss Winter?' He held up the pistol.

'Yes, Inspector.'

'Cor lumme, 'ow could I throw it away?' cried Nutty. 'I never 'ad it!'

'One moment, Mr. Potts,' said Hinton. 'Are you quite sure it was Mr. Potts and not Mr, Defoe, Miss Winter?'

'Mr. Macdonald was holding Mr. Defoe by then,' she answered, calmly. 'Mr. Potts was a little distance away. I don't think I could have been mistaken.'

'Blimey, I tell yer . . . '

'Did you actually see this pistol in Mr. Potts' hand?' asked Hinton, ignoring the outburst.

'Well . . . no, I didn't,' she admitted. 'It was too dark. But I saw him throw something away and, later, when I looked, I found the pistol.'

'That's right,' said Nutty, 'I did chuck something away. It was a button off Defoe's coat. It came off in me 'and when I collared 'im . . . '

'H'm,' said Hinton, thoughtfully. 'There is a button missing from Mr. Defoe's coat . . . '

''Course there is,' snapped Nutty, crossly. 'D'yer think I'm tellin' a pack o' ruddy lies? Cor lumme, what would I want ter shoot at Tangye for?'

'The same applies to me,' put in Defoe.

'*You?*' cried Nutty, scornfully. 'I wouldn't put nothin' past *you* after the dirty trick you played on us over the Rialter. What did yer come sneakin' in 'ere for, any'ow?'

'I've told you, I wished to see Mr. Brett.'

'What for, Mr. Defoe?' asked Hinton.

Phillip Defoe hesitated.

'Don't go thinkin' up no lies,' growled Nutty.

'It was a matter of business,' said Defoe, giving him an angry glance. 'I — I wished to make him an offer for a share in the show.'

'A share in the show — *this* show?' exclaimed Nutty. 'Cor stone me Aunt Clara! You've got a nerve, you 'ave. You chuck us out of yer perishin' theatre an' then, when everythin's goin' like a piece o' cake, you want a share in the show . . .'

'I was prepared to make Mr. Brett a business proposition,' said Defoe with an attempt at dignity.

'Thank you, we've had some of your business propositions,' said Brett, contemptuously.

Defoe flushed.

'There is no need to be insulting,' he retorted.

'We're rather getting away from the point,' broke in Hinton. 'The question is — who fired those shots at Miss Ward?'

'Well, it wasn't me,' declared Nutty.

'Or me,' said Defoe.

'Did you see anyone else near the back of the stalls who could have dropped that pistol, Miss Winter?' asked Hinton.

She shook her head. 'No,' she answered. She looked at Nutty. 'I'm sorry if I made a mistake . . . I certainly thought it was you . . . '

'O.K.,' he said with a grin. 'But it wasn't . . . '

'Can you suggest why anyone should want to injure Miss Ward?' asked the Inspector.

'Yes, I can,' said Keith, to their surprise. 'She has an idea of what may be behind all this . . . the murders and the rest of it . . . '

'She has, eh?' said Hinton with interest. 'What is her idea?'

'She thinks there is something hidden in the theatre,' said Keith. 'I think she's hit on the truth . . . '

'You think somebody knew what she

thought and got scared, eh?' said Hinton.

'Yes.'

'What does she think might be hidden here, Mr. Gilbert?'

'Something of value to the — the person who's responsible for all this,' answered Keith.

Hinton rubbed his chin gently. There was a peculiar look in his eyes.

'H'm,' he remarked after a pause. 'It's a plausible theory, anyway . . . '

'You've got to do something about it, Inspector,' said Keith, quickly. 'Miss Ward is in danger. There may be another and more successful attempt . . . '

'No, Mr. Gilbert,' said Hinton, shaking his head. 'I don't think you need worry about that . . . '

'You can't be sure . . . Not until you've got this unknown person under lock and key . . . '

'That won't be very long now,' remarked Hinton.

They all stared at him.

'Do you mean you know who it is?' demanded Brett.

'I've a very good idea,' said Hinton. He

looked from one to the other. 'Have you ever heard of a man called Harry Veeler?' he asked.

Macdonald uttered an exclamation.

'Harry Veeler?' he repeated.

'You look quite startled, Mr. Macdonald,' said Hinton. 'Does the name convey anything to you?'

# 20

During the next few days a great many
people were so busy that they had little
time for sleep. The postponement of the
dress rehearsal after the injury to Tangye
had involved Clifford Brett in a last-
minute rush. The date of the opening
night had already been announced in the
press and billing matter, and he did not
want to alter it. The tremendous amount
of publicity that both the theatre and the
show had received in the newspapers had
resulted in a rush to book seats directly
the box office was opened. The first night
was already sold out and there was a
steady demand for seats for several weeks
ahead. There was very little doubt that,
provided the show came up to the
public's expectations, they were in for a
success.

There were, as usual, a thousand and
one things to be done at the last minute.
Brett had arranged to have three dress

rehearsals to ensure that everything should go without a hitch on the opening night. This meant a great deal of work for everybody concerned, last-minute cutting and rearranging, alterations to dresses and scenery, and the dealing with unforeseen snags that cropped up.

Detective-Inspector Hinton was busy, too. The case was nearing its conclusion but, if the person responsible was not to slip through his fingers at the last moment, it required careful handling. The plan which he had mentioned to Boler was a good one, but it required working out in detail if it was to be successful. And it had to be successful. There would be no second opportunity if it misfired.

With the assistance of Sergeant Boler he perfected his plans, spending hours in the small and uncomfortable office at Scotland Yard pondering on the best method of approach. It was a difficult situation with which he was faced. He knew the criminal, but he had no proof. A false move and the guilty person would take alarm. The only way was to lay a trap — trap the killer in the act. To do this he had, in some way, to get an item of information to the suspect, but without making it look too obvious.

He puzzled over the problem and eventually he thought he had found a way . . .

Nutty Potts was busy, too.

He was trying to find some means of improving his relations with Maysie Sheringham. He called it 'improving', but secretly had to admit that, up to the present, he and Maysie had no relations at all. She just treated him as though he were something the cat had brought in. Nutty was fed up, but the girl attracted him, and he was determined not to give up . . .

Maysie Sheringham was busy, too.

Two of her dresses had to be entirely remade, which meant further visits to the dressmaker. The shoes for her finale dress had been overlooked. Rushing in and out of the theatre whenever she had a spare moment, she was annoyed to find Nutty always hovering about, obviously waiting an opportunity to speak. His eyes, as he gazed at her, reminded her of a dog who had been treated unkindly. She was so irritated that she wanted to scream . . .

Tangye was busy, too.

In the rush and anxiety of that hectic period she felt her nerves giving under the strain. She was quite sure that she was going to be a 'flop' and no amount of reassurance on the part of Keith and Brett could convince her otherwise. At the most stupid and ridiculous things, and for no reason at all, she found herself wanting to cry . . .

Angus Macdonald was busy, too.

He had many things to occupy his attention, and, while he sat at his desk and dealt with them, he found his mind wandering to that remark of Inspector Hinton's concerning Harry Veeler.

He was worried . . .

Olivia Winter was busy, too.

It was said that she practically ran the Macdonald Agency, and, to a large extent, this was true. Certainly she knew as much about the business as Macdonald, and took all the spade work off his shoulders. She spent most of her time telephoning the Regency, or acting as messenger between the theatre and the office.

She was so busy that she had little time to think about anything else . . .

And so, with everyone keyed up and working to the limit of their capacity, the first night drew on . . .

★   ★   ★

The new lights over the facia of the Regency blazed, shedding a golden glare over the stream of people that poured from private cars and taxis into the vestibule.

It was a fashionable first night. Many familiar faces were there and the constant flash of the camera bulbs was like continuous lightning.

There is something about the first night of a new show that has no parallel. You cannot find the same atmosphere at any other function — that peculiar blend of expectancy and excitement that crackles throughout audience and artists like an electric charge.

There was an added tension in the air

tonight, lacking in other first nights. This was the theatre where murder had stalked twice and every member of the huge audience was aware of it. There were many present who remembered the days of Castleton Mayne, one or two who had been in the theatre when he had met his tragic death. Would the same thing happen again? The newspapers had made much of the 'haunted theatre' and the slightly eerie feeling that hung in the air enhanced the pleasurable excitement.

There was nothing about the theatre itself to suggest tragedy. The old gilding had been restored, the clusters of pink shaded lights at intervals round circle and gallery shed a soft light over the old rose draperies. The huge chandelier from the centre of the roof was a-glitter with crystal. The rustle of dresses and programmes, and the hum of voices, reached beyond the great velvet tabs to the stage. Victor Price in dinner jacket and black tie, peered through a narrow gap at the slowly filling house. The orchestra pit below him was, as yet, empty. In the band-room under the stage the band were smoking a final pipe or cigarette, ignoring the large notice that prohibited this.

Price prayed, as he watched the audience trickling down the aisles to their seats, that the evening would go through without a hitch.

Tangye, already made up and dressed for her first entrance, sat in front of her dressing table, staring at her reflection in the big mirror. She felt sick. Her stomach seemed to be curling itself up in knots and she couldn't stop her hands from trembling. In a few minutes she would be out on the vast stage, focused in a blaze of light, with all those dim white blobs of faces spread out before her. Her throat was dry and stiff. She would never be able to utter more than a hoarse whisper. And she had to sing! The thought of it made her go hot. She could never do it — never! If only something would happen to postpone this dreadful ordeal. She sipped a glass of orange juice. It eased her throat for a second, but it soon went dry again. This, then, was fear. This was the nervous terror which she had heard about but never before experienced. It was different being in the chorus. She had felt nervous before, but not like this. Then she was only one among many — now she had to carry the greater part of the show on her own shoulders. She was largely responsible for its success or failure . . .

How often on other first nights had she envied the 'star'. Now she was one herself — the dream of her life realized — and she found nothing to envy. She would have given anything to run away and hide . . .

There was a tap on the door and Keith came in.

'Good luck, darling,' he said, stepping over and kissing the top of her head. 'You look lovely . . . '

'I feel awful,' she said in a voice that was husky and tremulous.

'Don't worry,' he said, patting her shoulder. 'You'll be all right. It's a wonderful house . . . '

'I hope I'm going to get through all right,' she said.

'Of course you are,' he said, reassuringly. 'The whole thing is going to be a terrible success . . . ' He had no idea of what the evening held in store. Perhaps it was as well that no premonition reached him.

'I do hope so,' said Tangye. 'Thank you for the lovely roses.' She looked at the enormous sheaf of red roses that he had sent.

Before he could reply the faint sound of a voice calling reached them: 'Overture and beginners, please . . . overture an' beginners . . . ' The sound of the call boy's voice drew nearer. Tangye's eyes grew panic-stricken.

'Oh!' she breathed.

There was a tap on the door and Brett put in his head. They could hear the distant music of the band.

'Good luck, Tangye,' he said. 'This is it. Keep your fingers crossed . . . '

'Thank you,' she answered. 'It's my legs I'm afraid of . . . '

'Nervous?' he said, smiling.

'Terribly.'

'You'll be all right — you've nothing to

worry about at all . . . '

'That's what I keep on telling her,' said Keith.

''Ullo, Tangye.' Nutty appeared round the open door. 'All the best . . . Lumme, yer do look nice.'

'The best of luck to all of you,' said Tangye.

'The overture's nearly finished,' said Brett. 'Are, you coming, Keith?'

'Yes . . . Bye-bye, darling . . . '

'Bye-bye, Keith . . . '

They went up to the stage. In the prompt corner, Price already has his finger on the warning bell for the tabs. Maysie Sheringham was just taking her place for the opening number. The overture came to its crashing conclusion, and there was a slight pause.

'All right, Miss Sheringham?' asked Price.

'Yes,' she answered.

'Good luck . . . good luck, girls.' He gave the signal to the band to start the introduction to the opening number. 'House lights,' he called, and pressed the warning bell. He took a quick look at the

299

stage to make sure that everyone was in their right place, and, as the orchestra reached the right bar in the music, pressed the bell to take up the tabs. They parted with a swish and swung up.

The show was on . . .

*   *   *

A few minutes before the curtain went up, Inspector Hinton took Olivia Winter aside in the vestibule.

'You thoroughly understand what we want you to do?' he said.

She nodded. Her expression was surprised and a little scared.

'Yes . . . I think so,' she said.

'You'll have to be very careful,' he said, gravely. 'Don't overdo it . . . Just mention it casually . . .'

'You can rely on me,' she answered, 'although I can scarcely believe that — that . . .'

He gave her a warning glance.

'Be careful,' he said, looking round quickly. 'I shouldn't say any more — in case we might be overheard . . .'

'Right! Tabs!' called Price. 'Kill those spots in that batten.'

There was a thunder of applause from the front as Tangye finished her first number and came off, breathless and flushed under her make-up.

'She's got 'em, Keith,' said Brett, delightedly. 'They like her.'

'Of course they do,' retorted Keith. 'She's good . . . That was grand, darling . . . '

'Fine, Tangye . . . You've got 'em eating out of your hand,' said Brett.

She smiled — a shaky little smile.

'It's lucky they couldn't see my knees,' she said. 'They were knocking like castanets . . . '

'You didn't sound a bit nervous.'

'But I was — terribly . . . I must go and change.' She hurried away . . .

★　★　★

Detective-Inspector Hinton and Detective-Sergeant Boler were enjoying the show from a side seat in the stalls. That is to say they were enjoying that part of it which a divided attention could take in. Their main attention was occupied in watching for the thing which had brought them there. The interval was drawing near when their vigilance might be rewarded.

'Our friend hasn't made a move yet,' whispered Hinton.

'Perhaps the bait isn't going to work?' muttered Boler.

'There we are,' broke in Hinton, suddenly. 'Look, making for the pass-door now . . . Come on . . . '

He slipped quietly out of his seat, and Boler followed him . . .

★ ★ ★

Angus Macdonald found Brett standing at the side watching the start of the finale to part one of the show.

'Ye've got a success, Brett,' he said. 'They're liking it well in front.'

'Yes,' agreed Clifford, 'it seems to be going well . . . '

'Aye, it is. It's a great show, and

302

Tangye's fine. I'm just going along to her dressing room to congratulate her. See ye in the bar, maybe?'

He made his way across the stage to the dressing rooms. A few minutes after he had gone, Olivia Winter appeared. 'Have you seen Mr. Macdonald?' she asked, anxiously.

Brett nodded.

'He's just gone along to Miss Ward's dressing room,' he answered.

'Oh . . . thank you.' She smiled and left him, a little abruptly he thought.

Price, hot and flustered from an altercation with a stage hand, came up.

'We're running a bit late, Victor,' warned Brett, looking at his watch.

'I know,' answered the harassed stage manager. 'Only six minutes, though. I'll try and make that up in the second half . . . ' He grabbed hold of the call boy. 'Go and call Miss Sheringham, Dan . . . '

'It's all right, Victor, I'm here,' said Maysie, coming up behind them.

There was a sudden blare of music.

'You're on, Miss Sheringham,' said Price. 'Lights, second set of tabs . . . '

* * *

Half hidden behind a pile of scenery, Hinton and Boler stood waiting.

'Any minute now, I think,' murmured the Inspector.

Boler strained his eyes to pierce the gloom.

'I can't see very well,' he said.

Hinton stood silent. Would the bait work? Would this dangerous fish rise to it? No sign yet and the time was passing. Would the person he was after leave it until later on? Some move would *have* to be made soon. Otherwise it would be too late . . .

A movement . . . A figure came out of the shadows by the iron door and began to walk stealthily towards the ladder leading to the flies.

The bait *had* worked!

# 21

The murderer began to climb the ladder.

'Come on, sir,' whispered Boler, urgently.

'No, no — wait,' said Hinton, restraining him. 'We'll spoil everything if we're too soon . . . '

The figure on the ladder climbed slowly upwards until it was lost to view in the shadows of the flies.

'Now,' whispered Hinton.

They left the concealing scenery and made their way cautiously over to the iron ladder. The finale to the first half of the revue was still going on, and the stage hands were all grouped downstage watching. They had the place to themselves.

'Be careful how you go,' said Hinton, as he began to mount the ladder. 'Keep behind me and don't make any noise . . . '

Silently they went up, rung by rung. The ladder was narrow and fixed close to the wall, by no means an easy climb to anyone unused to it. Presently they came to the 'catwalk'. Ahead of them, moving cautiously along the narrow gangway, was the person they were after. In the wall of the theatre, at the other end of the 'catwalk' was a dark, oblong opening. It was, as Hinton very well knew, a ventilator. Towards it the figure they were following was making its way.

They stopped, watching and praying that their quarry would not look round. The figure of the murderer reached the oblong recess and started to feel about inside.

It was then that Hinton acted.

'You're wasting your time,' he said, sternly. 'The Easthanger emeralds are not there.'

The figure uttered a gasp of surprise and fear and swung round to face them.

It was Olivia Winter!

'Oh!' she said, recovering partially from her first shock. 'I don't know what you mean, Inspector . . .'

'Oh, yes you do,' snapped Hinton. 'Your real name is Olivia Veeler and you are the sister of Harry Veeler who was killed just after he had succeeded, with your help, in escaping from prison, where he was serving a sentence for stealing the Duchess of Easthanger's emeralds. I'm arresting you for the murder of Alexander Mayne, the murder of Madeleine Peters, the murder of Detective-Sergeant James Savernick, and the attempted murder of Tangye Ward. I warn you that anything you say . . . '

The face of the woman on the narrow 'catwalk' changed. It became the face of a devil.

'Keep back!' she spat at them between her teeth, and snatched a tiny automatic from her bag. 'Don't come any nearer and don't touch me. If you do I'll shoot . . . '

'Put that pistol away!' snapped Hinton.

Her lips curled back from her teeth in a snarl.

'I mean what I say,' she said. 'Don't come any nearer . . . '

'This won't do you any good,' said Hinton.

'Won't it?' she grated. 'You think you're clever, but you haven't caught me yet

. . . Keep away, I tell you!' Her voice rose as he took a step forward. 'I'll shoot if you move . . . '

It was Boler who saw the great canvas backcloth swishing down from the dark grid above them. It was coming within a few inches of them. It couldn't fail to hit the arm of the woman — the arm crooked over the low rail and holding the tiny pistol . . .

'Look out!' he cried. 'Mind that bit o' scenery . . . '

'Do you think you can catch me with an old trick like that?' she began, and then the heavy batten at the bottom of the cloth struck her. She gave a startled cry, lost her balance, tried desperately to recover it, and fell from the 'catwalk' to the stage fifty feet below.

★   ★   ★

Victor Price heard the thud of her body as it struck the stage, above the music.

'What the heck was that noise?' he demanded angrily, leaving the prompt corner. A startled stage hand met him as he hurried round a massive set.

'It's a woman, sir,' said the man, jerking his head over his shoulder. 'Fell from the flies, she did . . . '

'A woman?' repeated Price. 'What the . . . ?'

'Can't you make less noise there?' snapped Brett, joining them. 'They'll hear you out in front if . . . ' He caught sight of the crumpled heap on the stage. 'Good God! What's happened?'

'She fell from the . . . It's Miss Winter!'

They hurried over to the body. She lay on her back, her legs bent under her. She was moaning faintly and there was blood on her lips. A group of curious stage hands and a few members of the company gathered round.

'She's pretty badly hurt,' muttered Brett. 'How did it happen?'

Price shook his head.

'I've no idea,' he said. 'I heard the thud, that's all . . . '

'She fell from the flies,' said the stage hand. 'I saw it 'appen. Dropped like a stone, she did.' He gave his information with relish.

'What was she doing up there?' demanded Brett. 'Oh, well, never mind that now. We ought to get a doctor . . . '

'Is she dead?' Inspector Hinton hurried up breathlessly.

'No . . . how did it happen?' asked Brett.

'A piece of scenery hit her and knocked her off the gangway up there,' said Hinton, dropping on one knee beside the injured woman.

'But . . . what was she doing up there?' demanded the bewildered stage manager. 'She'd no right . . . '

'She was responsible for the murders and all the rest of it,' said Hinton, curtly.

'What, Miss Winter?' cried Brett, incredulously.

'Her real name is Veeler,' answered Hinton.

Price suddenly remembered something.

'Good Lord, you must get her away from there,' he said. 'We've got to take this cloth up in a few seconds . . . if you leave her there she'll be seen from the audience . . . '

'Take her to Miss Ward's dressing

room,' said Brett. 'There's a settee there . . . '

'You go and ring up the station, Boler,' ordered Hinton. 'Ask them to send round the Divisional Surgeon at once . . . '

The Sergeant nodded and hurried away.

'Be careful how you lift her,' began Hinton, and was interrupted by the stage hand.

'Cor lumme,' exclaimed the man, 'look at this.' He pointed to a sandbag on the stage near them. It was one of the sandbags which are used to weight the sets of lines that hoist the backcloths. 'It fell with 'er, an' bust open . . . but this ain't sand, it looks like — like some sort o' green glass . . . '

In one stride Hinton was over and staring down at the burst sandbag. 'The Easthanger emeralds,' he said, softly. 'Queer that. She found 'em after all . . . '

★ ★ ★

Clifford Brett came quickly along the passage towards Tangye's dressing room.

311

The show was nearly over. He was almost at the door when it opened and Hinton came out.

'It's all over,' he said.

'You mean she's dead?' asked Brett.

The Inspector nodded.

'Yes,' he answered. 'We managed to get a statement from her. I rather think Mr. Defoe will have some explaining to do . . . '

'Defoe?' Brett looked his surprise.

'She told us why Madeleine Peters was here that night,' said Hinton. 'She came to set fire to the theatre . . . '

'Set fire — to the theatre?' echoed Brett.

'The idea was Defoe's. He'd had a special sort of incendiary bomb made — with a time fuse. Madeleine Peters was sent to plant it. She discovered Winter, or Veeler to give her her right name, in the theatre and . . . Well, you know what happened to her . . . '

'Why on earth did Defoe want to set fire to the theatre?' asked Brett.

'If you hadn't a theatre he thought he could buy up the show cheaply,' answered

Hinton. 'Peters told Veeler the whole plot before she was killed. You hadn't got the scenery in then. Defoe thought he could get the whole thing, lock, stock and barrel, for a song . . . '

'Nice little scheme,' commented Brett. 'Of course that didn't suit Olivia Veeler's books at all. She didn't want the theatre set on fire. She hadn't found the emeralds. If the place was burned down, she never would find them.'

'So she killed Madeleine Peters, eh?'

'Yes, she *had* to,' said Hinton. 'When Peters found her here she knew that she was the person who had killed Mayne.'

'How did *you* know that it was Olivia Win — er Veeler?'

'I guessed it might be when she told that story about the man who came to the office and left that knife,' replied Hinton. 'It could only have been a lie or a miracle . . . I don't believe in miracles . . . '

'I see . . . yes, I suppose we were all very dense over that,' said Brett. 'I suppose she discovered the secret of the sealed room from Mrs. Mayne?'

'Yes, she saw the old lady work it one

night — when she brought fresh flowers. It proved very useful to her. There was always a place to hide if she was disturbed during one of her periodical searches.'

'What I don't understand,' said Brett, 'is how she knew where to look for the emeralds tonight?'

Hinton smiled.

'I was responsible for that,' he said. 'You see, I knew the story of Harry Veeler and the robbery, and the relationship between him and the woman who called herself Olivia Winter. I was sure that she was the person we wanted, but I couldn't have proved it. The fact that she was Veeler's sister wouldn't have cut much ice in a court. She would have said that she changed her name because of her brother's reputation. There was nothing to prove that she even knew anything about the emeralds.

'Of course it would have looked very suspicious, but suspicion isn't proof. You've to have a cast-iron case to put before a jury. So I invented a story to tell her. I said that we had found out that a man called Harry Veeler had hidden the proceeds of a robbery — the Easthanger emeralds — in a ventilator in the flies. I said that one of his fellow convicts had given us the information. Veeler had told him about it before he escaped. I told her that we thought the emeralds were at the root of all the trouble in the theatre, and I hinted that we suspected Macdonald . . . '

'Macdonald?' exclaimed Brett.

'Yes. You see I had to get the information to her without letting her think it was intended for her, if you see what I mean?'

'I think I do,' said Brett. 'Go on.'

'Our only chance was to catch her red-handed, so to speak. I knew that if she thought we had found the emeralds she would make an attempt to get them and give herself away. I asked her if she would mention casually to Mr. Macdonald that we had found the emeralds. I told her that they were where Harry Veeler had hidden them — in the ventilator. I said that we hadn't removed them and I implied that we were keeping a close watch on Mr. Macdonald . . . '

'It sounds a pretty thin story to me,' remarked Brett.

'It did to me,' confessed Hinton. 'But she fell for it. I knew she wouldn't say anything to Mr. Macdonald and I was sure that she would try and get hold of the emeralds herself at the first opportunity. From her point of view it was her last chance, you see? She'd gone too far not to take one further risk to get them. At least that's how I worked it out, and I was right . . . '

'That was a hell of a risk on her part,' said Brett.

'Not the way she looked at it,' said Hinton. 'She had no idea we had connected her with Veeler. She thought we would be concentrating our attention on Macdonald. What she had to do would only take a few seconds, or so she thought.'

'What made her kill your man, Savernick?' said Brett. 'I suppose she was responsible for that, too?'

'Oh, yes, she was responsible for that,' answered Hinton. 'I think he had got on to her — of course I'm only guessing, but

I think that is what it was. She heard him beginning to say what he knew over the telephone. She acted quickly and . . . that was the end of poor Savernick.'

'She certainly had nerve,' said Brett.

'Yes, I think, perhaps, this is the best ending,' said Hinton. 'She might have got away with it after all. Juries are funny things.' He rubbed his chin gently. 'That was a queer coincidence,' he said, 'about those emeralds in the sandbag. One of the shots she fired as she was knocked over the rail hit it. Very queer that . . . '

The faint voice of the call boy reached them.

'All down for the finale, please . . . all down for the finale . . . all down for the finale, please . . . '

'Good Lord, the show's nearly over,' exclaimed Brett. 'I must get back up to the stage . . . '

He turned and hurried away along the passage.

The voice of the call boy grew louder.

'All down for the finale, please . . . all down for the finale . . . '

Hinton stood for a moment watching

him as he came nearer and nearer, shouting and banging on the dressing room doors. Then he turned and went into the room where Sergeant Boler was keeping a watch over the dead woman.

# 22

The show was a bigger success than they had dared to hope. At the final fall of the curtain the huge audience stood up and cheered themselves hoarse. Tangye had to take seven curtain calls before they were satisfied.

When the curtain came down for the last time, Keith went up to the flushed and tearful girl.

'Darling,' he said, 'you're wonderful . . . wonderful!'

She looked at him through her tears.

'I hope you'll always think so,' she said.

The supper party which Clifford Brett had arranged at the Milan was a gay affair. The enormous success of the show had put everybody concerned in the highest spirits, and even the tragedy which had happened in their midst was forgotten. The shadow of fear which hung over the theatre was gone for good — gone with the passing of the woman who had been responsible for it.

'We'll open up the sealed dressing room,' said Brett. 'I'll arrange for the workmen to come in at once. We'll have a new door put in, and the whole place thoroughly cleaned and redecorated . . . '

'I doubt if ye'll get anybody to use it,' remarked Macdonald. 'Theatre people are a superstitious crowd.'

'I'm not suggesting that it should be used as a dressing room again,' said Brett. 'I'm going to have it fitted up as an office. It'll be more convenient than having to go round to the front of the house.'

'By the way,' said Macdonald, 'I forgot to tell ye in all the excitement. Mrs. Duppy came to the office today. She wants a job. Now that Mrs. Mayne's dead she's nothing to do, poor old soul. I was wonderin' . . . '

'Send her along to see me,' said Brett. 'We could do with an extra dresser. She'll feel more at home at the Regency than anywhere else, I should think . . . '

'I'll have to find a new secretary,' remarked Macdonald. He sighed. 'I shall miss Olivia Winter. Whatever she was she was a good secretary . . . '

'And a thoroughly dangerous woman,' said Brett.

Nutty Potts, further down the table, turned to Maysie. By a clever piece of strategy he had succeeded in sitting next to her.

'Well,' he said, 'I've asked yer often enough to 'ave a meal with me, an' 'ere we are at last — eatin' at the same table . . . '

She smiled.

'I couldn't very well help it, could I?' she said.

'Lumme,' he exclaimed, 'that's a nice thin' ter say, that is . . . '

'What would you like me to say?' she asked.

'You might be a bit matey,' he answered. 'I mean, if I said, 'What about a bit o' lunch tergether tomorrer' you might say: 'Thanks, Nutty' or something like that.'

'Thanks, Nutty,' she said.

He looked at her, his eyes round with surprise.

''Ere,' he said, 'say that again.'

'Thanks, Nutty,' she repeated obligingly.

'D'yer really mean it?' he said. 'Will yer 'ave lunch with me tomorrer?'

'I should like to very much,' she answered.

He was so astonished that all he could say was: 'Blimey!'

★　★　★

Phillip Defoe walked slowly across the tarmac to the waiting plane. His face was as grey as the sky above him. All his plans had crashed about his ears and he was trying to crawl away from the wreckage. His financial position for the past few months had been worse than he had hinted to Madeleine Peters. To pay all he owed would take many times the money he still had left. There was nothing for it but to go — while the going was good. In the briefcase which he carried was every penny he could lay his hands on — amounting to some four thousand pounds. It wasn't much but it would give him a start in another country.

He walked up the gangway and took his seat.

The rain which had been threatening began to fall as the plane took off. He looked out of the window as they left the runway. The aerodrome grew smaller, a tiny, model-like thing, rapidly disappearing in the grey curtains of rain . . . Presently it vanished altogether and there was nothing but a mist of cloud . . .

## THE END

GRIM DEATH
MURDER IN MANUSCRIPT
THE GLASS ARROW
THE THIRD KEY
THE ROYAL FLUSH MURDERS
THE SQUEALER
MR. WHIPPLE EXPLAINS
THE SEVEN CLUES
THE CHAINED MAN
THE HOUSE OF THE GOAT
THE FOOTBALL POOL MURDERS
THE HAND OF FEAR
SORCERER'S HOUSE
THE HANGMAN
THE CON MAN
MISTER BIG
THE JOCKEY
THE SILVER HORSESHOE
THE TUDOR GARDEN MYSTERY

We do hope that you have enjoyed reading this large print book.

Did you know that all of our titles are available for purchase?

We publish a wide range of high quality large print books including:
**Romances, Mysteries, Classics**
**General Fiction**
**Non Fiction and Westerns**

Special interest titles available in large print are:
**The Little Oxford Dictionary**
**Music Book, Song Book**
**Hymn Book, Service Book**

Also available from us courtesy of Oxford University Press:
**Young Readers' Dictionary**
**(large print edition)**
**Young Readers' Thesaurus**
**(large print edition)**

For further information or a free brochure, please contact us at:
**Ulverscroft Large Print Books Ltd.,**
**The Green, Bradgate Road, Anstey,**
**Leicester, LE7 7FU, England.**
**Tel:** (00 44) 0116 236 4325
**Fax:** (00 44) 0116 234 0205

# THE SILVER HORSESHOE

## Gerald Verner

John Arbinger receives an anonymous note — offering 'protection' from criminal gangs in exchange for £5,000 — with the impression of a tiny silver horseshoe in the bottom right-hand corner. Ignoring the author's warning about going to the police, Arbinger seeks the help of Superintendent Budd of Scotland Yard. But Budd is too late to save Arbinger from the deadly consequences of his actions, and soon the activities of the Silver Horseshoe threaten the public at large — as well as the lives of Budd and his stalwart companions . . .

# A MURDER MOST MACABRE

## Edmund Glasby

Jeremy Lavelle, leader of the esoteric Egyptian Society the Order of the True Sphinx, has illegally purchased an ancient Egyptian mummy. Watched by his enthralled followers, he opens the coffin and begins to unwrap the body . . . The head is that of an ancient scribe, his shrivelled and desiccated face staring eyelessly up from his coffin — yet from the neck down, wrapped up in layers of bandages, are not the mummified remains which they had expected. Instead, they stare in horror at the decapitated corpse of a recently killed man!